# HOLIDAY FLING

## J. SAMAN

# Faina

"You're either a holiday lover or you're not." That's what my boyfriend said to me when he dragged me out the door tonight, dressed in my preholiday best. A red dress and matching heels and lipstick. I'm an inbetweener though that wasn't an acceptable answer.

But when you have no parents and no extended family beyond your twin sister, who married a billionaire and likes to travel the world over Christmas, the holidays aren't all that great. More often than not, I've spent Christmas with my television and Chinese takeout.

But honestly, that's just sort of how it is, and I've come to accept it.

This year, however, is different. This year I have my boyfriend, Brooks. As it's three days out from Christmas and our office is shut down until after the new year, I have seven days of quiet bliss, wrapped up in his super nice apartment—since mine is being fumigated for an unfortunate pest situation.

Sounds pretty damn great to me. Even if it means attending social functions, like our office holiday party tonight.

My bags are packed and waiting in the trunk of my car, and Brooks told me he already cleared out two drawers and a row in his closet for me. It's only been eight months since Brooks hired me to be the chief marketing and public relations director of All That Media. It was a bit of back and forth between us, but after about three months, we started dating, and it's been a slice of pie away from heaven ever since.

"What do you think, babe?" he asks as we step into the pretty ballroom he rented out for tonight at the Ritz in Boston. "Looks great, right?"

"It's amazing," I exclaim as I look around, taking it all in. "I love it. You did a brilliant job with the space."

Lots of pretty gold fairy lights and two tall Christmas trees are fully decorated, and the tables are lined with red tablecloths, white roses, orchids, and votives. It's beautiful and romantic. The event coordinator did a fantastic job, and it was well worth all the extra late-night sessions Brooks put in with her. All our big clients are here tonight, and it's *the* event before everything officially shuts down for the holidays.

He gives me a preening smile and then dives in to steal a quick kiss. "Love you." He gives me a wink and then swoops up two glasses of champagne for us from a passing server. "Here. Tip it back and let's have some fun."

Brooks and I hit the dance floor for a while, and then I end up chatting with some friends from the marketing department while Brooks finds himself being called away by the event coordinator to deal with some catering issues. Whatever the issue is, it carries on until cocktail hour is over and dinner is getting ready to begin.

"Where is Brooks?" our CFO questions, rushing over to me in a tizzy, her expression frantic. "He's supposed to make the keynote speech before dinner, and I can't find him anywhere."

People are being called to their tables, still preoccupied enough that I have a few minutes if I hurry. "I'll go look for him."

"Here."

She hands me the microphone he needs for his speech, and I scooter around, going from the bar to the bathroom to the kitchen, but I can't find him anywhere. It isn't until I leave the ballroom and walk along the corridor, heading back toward the entrance of the hotel that I hear two people arguing from an alcove beside the ballroom entrance.

"You told me you'd talk to her about it. You told me this would all be done before Christmas."

"I can't do that," Brooks snarls. "She has no place to go. They're doing something to her apartment."

"I've been letting you fuck me for weeks! You promised me you'd break up with her by now."

That makes my steps falter, and I practically trip over my own feet as I slink over to the wall a few feet from them. I can't see them. But I sure as hell can hear them. My arm presses into the wall, and I hold myself up with it. The microphone slips from my hand, dropping to the carpet with a dull thud. Only they don't hear it as they're too busy fighting.

"Shhh," he hisses. "Keep your voice down. This isn't the time or place for that."

"Oh, but it was fine enough for you to stick your dick in my mouth."

Jesus. A cold sweat breaks out across my forehead as my vision grows fuzzy. The two glasses of champagne I consumed during cocktail hour churn violently in my stomach.

"You dragged me out here, practically begging for it. Now I have to get back inside. We both do. This is a big event, and I know my absence won't go unnoticed for long."

"No," the woman half-shouts with urgency as he starts to leave the alcove, only for her hand to reach out and grab his tuxedo jacket, yanking him back in. "Brooks, we need to figure this out now. You made promises. It's the only reason I started this with you. After tonight, we no longer have an excuse to see each other, and I'm not letting it end like that. I want to spend the holidays with you."

He makes an annoyed noise. "Listen, you need to get over that. It can't happen. Faina is staying with me through New Year's. I can't kick her out, and I already promised her she could."

"I don't care. You also told me you wanted to be with me."

He grunts. "I do. It just isn't the right time for us."

"So you'd rather spend your holidays with *her*?" She's incredulous, her voice growing louder.

"Stop, already," he hisses, trying to quiet her down. "We have to get back."

"You told me you didn't love her," she continues, not slowing or calming down. "You said the sex with her was horrible. That she's so bland and unadventurous, she even manages to make vanilla bored with her."

Oh god. He said that about me? To the woman he's currently screwing? My face burns with humiliation, and I press my back against the wall, trying to catch my breath. What have I been doing for the last five months with him? I work with him. He's my boss and this job… it's my dream job.

"I know I said that about her, and I know the sex between you and me has been fun, but I'm not breaking up with Faina. She's the best PR and marketing director I've ever had. All my clients love her. You'll have to get over it, or just, you know, move on."

She emits a shrill noise. "Fun?! Move on?! Are you kidding me? You're not ending this with me. I could do her job. Something you promised me I'd get when you broke up with her!" The woman stomps her heeled foot.

A cold sweat breaks out on my forehead. I can't believe what I'm hearing. I can't believe all the things he said to her, the promises he made at my expense. He's been telling me he loves me. He made room in his fucking closet for me! All the while he's been screwing her behind my back for *weeks*, and I had no clue.

Scalding tears burn the backs of my eyes and the tip of my nose, and I suck down deep breaths that do nothing to calm me.

I hear a rustling, but I can't see it to know what it is. "That's not going to happen, Kim. I only said all of that to get you into bed. Frankly, all I wanted was the sex. You should have figured out I was done with you when I walked in with Faina on my arm tonight. Now you need to get over it and be a professional, or I'll destroy your career and reputation. You got it? We're done here, and I'm done with you."

I right my body, wanting to get out of here and away from him before I have to face them. I'm not ready for that big blowout yet, and it's certainly not something I want to do here in front of all these people. Only, in doing so, I accidentally kick the microphone into the wall. It makes that horrific, shrieky feedback noise microphones make.

When they're on.

Brooks and Kim, the event coordinator, shoot out of their alcove to find me standing there.

"Faina! Shit." Brooks starts for me only to stop short, his hands outstretched as if he's going to try and touch me, only to think better of it when he reads from my face that I heard everything. Well, minus the dick-sucking action. Thank God for that. It would have given me nightmares for weeks.

His dark eyes are wild, unsure of what to do or how to proceed. Kim, meanwhile, looks like she doesn't know what to do with herself or how to feel. She just got publicly dumped by the guy she wants, but in the same turn, so did his girlfriend.

I bend down and pick up the microphone, bringing it to my mouth, already knowing that everything Brooks and Kim said—all the cheating and comments about how boring and horrible I am in bed—played through the speakers in the ballroom.

I guess it's too late to run, so I might as well roll with it and try to preserve some of my dignity.

"Ladies and gentlemen." My voice trembles, and I clear it. "We are so delighted you could join us this evening. I hope you're all enjoying yourselves as well as the pre-dinner entertainment provided to you by none other than the CEO himself, Brooks Loftin. Mr. Loftin, your audience is ready for your speech. Well, your second one, that is."

I thrust the microphone at him, his face burning with fury, but it's not like I called him a womanizing, soul-sucking piece of shit or anything who deserves the world's largest piece of coal in his stocking. Actually, I think I handled that tactfully and full of grace.

Considering I want to rip him apart with my bare hands until he bleeds and cries like a little girl.

I almost feel sorry for Kim. I mean, she knew she was screwing around with a taken guy, and that drags her down several notches in the women's empowerment guidebook, but we both put our faith and trust in the same guy only to be fucked over by him in the end.

Brooks takes the microphone from my hand, and I give him a coy smile I don't even come close to feeling as I saunter over to him. He gives me a wary look, clearly unsure of what my intentions are. Just as I get close enough, I knee him straight in the balls.

He makes a delightful oomph sound, his body doubling over from the pain.

I pat his back. "I really hope that hurt and did some permanent damage." Then I turn to her. "He's all yours now."

I push past her, heading for the exit, and when I breach the partition between the event space and the lobby of the hotel, I give up on trying to be brave and race into the bar, collapsing into a vacant seat and covering my mouth to stifle my sobs.

Oh my God. I can't believe he was cheating on me. For weeks. And who knows if that was the first time? Thank God we never had sex without a condom. But... the things he said about me. My face heats all over again as tears start to leak, falling onto my cheeks.

I admit, the sex wasn't all that fun or adventurous.

Maybe that was on me. I don't know. I was never all that into it with him. I just never felt... excited when I was with him.

All I know is I have no place to go because I can't go home, and after the first of the year, I won't have a job either. I'm a cliché. I'm an office cliché. Humiliated in front of everyone, not just coworkers but clients too.

How can I ever show my face in this city again after that?

"Miss, are you all right?" I blink through my tears and glance up at the waiter standing over me.

"No. My boyfriend is a philanderer. Do you have anything for that?"

He gives me a wan smile. "Actually, I do. Don't move."

I'm about to say I won't because I have nowhere else to go, but he's already gone, hopefully having the bartender whip me up something magical. I slide out my phone, leaning forward and resting my elbows on my thighs as I stare at my screen.

I can't stay with anyone from work after what happened tonight, and my college best friend is away for the week along with our other best friend. They had invited me to go with them, and I declined so I could stay with fucking Brooks for the week and do Christmas with him. They're on a cruise, and it's not exactly like you can just hop on board mid-sailing and join.

So where does that leave me?

"Here you go." The bartender places the largest martini I've ever seen in my life in front of me. The thing looks like one of those novelty items you'd find in a gag store. It's easily five times the size of a regular martini glass.

I sit up, cackling out a wet laugh. "Where on earth did you get a glass that size?"

"They were a misorder that came in a few weeks ago. We saved a few as a joke."

I blink at it and then look up to him. "Thank you. I think this might be perfect."

"You're welcome. But I'm going to call you an Uber home if you drink even half of that."

I eyeball the glass filled with pink liquid. "You've got a deal."

He hands me a straw—because it's too big to lift or even tilt—and I drop it in the glass, taking a long pull and swallowing down multiple sips. it's delicious and fruity without being too sweet.

"Good?" he asks.

"Orgasmic." Not that I'd know. "Thank you again."

"My pleasure. Sorry about your boyfriend."

I give him a sad smile, and then he goes back to work, and I make the call I've been dreading. The phone rings and rings, and just when I don't think Ava is going to pick up, she proves me wrong.

"Hey, what's up?" she says into the phone. The last time I spoke to her was a few weeks ago, but it's been strained between us since Brooks and I got together. She was the one to remind me about the cliché, and I fought with her over it because I was stupid enough to believe it would never happen to me. I'm about to get an *I told you so* I am in no mood for.

I take another sip of my drink, needing the alcohol to get through this. "You were right."

It's all I have to say, but it still takes her a second to grasp my meaning, and then she sucks in a sharp breath. "Oh, shit, Fai. I'm sorry. I won't say I told you so, but—"

"Ava, I swear, I will never speak to you again if you say it."

She sighs. "Fine. I won't say it. What did the bastard do, and do you want me to hire a hitman to kill him? I live in LA, and Will knows people. It's not beyond the realm of possibility."

"Tonight, at the event, I overheard him fighting with the other woman." I explain everything from what he said to how the microphone was on, and by the end, my sister is laughing her ass off.

"You are my hero! I can't believe you did that. You don't need to hire an assassin. You *are* the assassin."

"Well, the dickface had it coming and then some. But now I'm homeless, jobless, and mortified beyond belief. Everyone heard what he said about me. You know the sort of clients we have and how bad that is for my name and reputation. Now it's three days before Christmas and I'll never be able to find anything affordable for the week. Can I come and crash with you and Will wherever you're going for Christmas?"

Will is Ava's high school sweetheart. We all grew up together in California. Will is the son of an LA-based shipping mogul. Ava and I grew up on the non-wealthy side of LA, our parents were teachers at an exclusive prep school, so we got to attend for free. Ava and Will married straight out of college, and now they never stay anywhere longer than they have to. Last I spoke to her, they were in Taiwan, but she told me they were going to spend Christmas in the US.

She makes a noise. "Actually, we're staying in LA. Will has the flu. Woke up with it this morning, and the doctor confirmed it."

I puff out a stricken breath. "Oh, I'm so sorry, Ava. How's Will feeling?"

"Like total crap. He has a fever and a nasty cough."

"I hope he's okay."

"He'll be fine. It just puts our holiday plans on hold," she says, her voice growing somber. "I'd invite you here, but with him having the flu, I don't want to risk you getting sick. We were going to be staying in Jackson Hole for the holiday. We rented a place up there that we're not going to be able to use now. It's yours if you want it."

"Jackson Hole?" I scrunch up my nose.

"Yes, Fai. As in Wyoming. It's cold but beautiful, with lots of snow and holiday cheer, and some of the best skiing there is."

I snort. "Skiing? Do you know me at all?"

"Okay, fine, no skiing for you, but it's a good place to go and lick your wound.

It's about as off-the-grid and different from Boston as you can get. And your asshat of a boss-slash-ex lover will never find you there."

She might have a point with that. And frankly, I'm out of options. I can go and hide away in a mountain lodge or whatever they rented for a week while I figure out what I'm going to do next.

"I guess Jackson Hole it is."

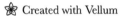 Created with Vellum

## Chapter One

Dex

IF IT WERE UP to me, I'd blow up the entire month of December. All the lights and trees and lovely decorations. All the cheerful advertisements with puppies and children and fake Santas. The incessant holiday carols that are pumped into the atmosphere with the sole design to repeat forever in your brain. It's not that I hate Christmas necessarily, in fact, in years past, I've rather enjoyed it.

But this year, two things happened.

One, my mum passed away about five months ago, which left an unhealable chasm in my chest. Two, I had a really bad night roughly two weeks ago that resulted in me getting arrested for assault. In fairness, I don't regret breaking the nose of the man who was in my bed fucking my fiancée. Twenty-four hours later, my now ex-fiancée released a sex tape of me screwing another woman while I was still with my fiancée.

Before you go and judge, it was a threesome designed and led by my fiancée who told me she thought it would be so hot and fun and that it was one of her ultimate fantasies. She begged me to do it. I was dumb. I was in love—or so I thought —and wanted to make my woman happy by giving her everything she ever desired.

Again, I was dumb. And clearly far too trusting.

It's put me in a bit of a bind with my record label who are less than thrilled with all the negative press.

Especially when the incidents hit front-page news not only across the UK but across the world. Then I dropped the cherry of all cherries on top of my ice cream sundae. I fired my PR manager. Stupid? Probably, but considering my fiancée was my PR manager, I didn't exactly have a choice. She played me like a maestro and kept the video for retaliation, ready to exploit me at the most opportune moment.

And that moment was when I caught her actually cheating and reacted and then fired her. My name—my reputation— it's all fucked thanks to her and her lies. No one wants to hear my side of it because she looks like the victim—the woman is in PR and knows how to spin a good story—and I look like the womanizing, violent, loose cannon.

As my best mate Will put it rather bluntly, I need to hide out for a while.

And as misery would have it, Will woke up yesterday with the flu. With that, his plans for a winter holiday with his wife were put on hold. He begged me to take over his rental in the States. Promised it was the perfect spot to take a break, let the news simmer down, and work on some new music.

So now here I am in bloody Wyoming of all places, and after nearly fifteen hours of travel, including a stop to refuel, I pull up in front of the house in my rental SUV and park in the driveway. That was a trip, driving on the wrong side of the road—something I haven't done in years since I primarily live in London and not LA now. Light snow dances gently from the heavens, making the small cabin-style home tucked at the end of the long road, framed by mountains and fir trees, all the more picturesque.

There's nothing for miles. No sound other than the wind gently rustling the branches of the trees. No reporters hiding in the shrubbery outside my flat. It's pristine and beautiful and perfectly peaceful out here. It's also more snow than I've ever seen in my life, and as I step out of my car, I take a deep inhale of the cold, clean air.

My insides immediately calm, shifting into a quieter pace for the first time in I can't even remember how long. This is what I needed. To get away and relax. To forget the nightmare my ex put me through and focus on myself. On my music.

And pray my problems resolve themselves somehow.

With the first smile on my face in two weeks, I pull my luggage out of the boot and then make my way up to the front door. I punch in the code on the lock, already knowing this place is going to be above all when I get inside since that's how Will and Ava travel.

The lock makes a delightful chirp, and then I pull the lever and step inside to what can only be described as a quintessential Christmas in the mountains escape. The charming open area boasts a massive top-of-the-line kitchen complete with the biggest island I've ever seen. Nearby is a large oval dining table, already set for eight. Off to the side is a library with windows on all sides, and a desk that holds two monitors. The two-story sitting area is a conglomerate of brown leather and soft cream fabrics with a towering stone fireplace. There's a colossal, fully decorated Christmas tree that practically touches the ceiling, and Christmas lights and decorations cover every inch, though done quite tastefully.

Will had mentioned the back of the cabin has a second seating room with an additional fireplace that leads to an outdoor area with a whirlpool tub that I can't wait to check out. The views through the windows in the kitchen and great room are a continuation of the landscape I already got an eyeful of outside.

For a moment, I just stand here, taking it all in until small things start to spark at me. Like there's a fire half-attempted in the fireplace, the logs charred and smoking with no flame, and the scent of freshly baked cookies lingers in the air, that is clearly from the plate of decorated sugar cookies sitting on the counter. But it's the dishes in the drying rack that give me pause and have me squinting around, taking in other small things that suggest someone has been here rather recently.

Like the bottles of wine and spirits on the counter by the sink and the beep of the coffee maker when it finishes brewing its pot.

Will never mentioned a housekeeper, though that doesn't surprise me considering he and Ava go first class with all the luxury and perks wherever they are.

"Hello?" I call out, though I hear nothing, and no one responds. Will must have informed the housekeeper I was coming, and she popped over early to make me coffee and cookies. And deliver alcohol, which he knew I'd need.

I snicker a bit at that as I wheel my luggage toward the stairs and then carry it up.

The master suite—which is the only bedroom here it appears—takes up the entire second floor with yet another fireplace and a large dark wood, four-poster king-size bed, and more grand windows. But as I enter the room, I stop short when I find women's clothes strewn across the chair in the corner. Black yoga pants, a white pullover, and a very thin and lacy white bra with matching knickers.

*What in the hell?*

"Hello? I call out a second time, only to catch the sound of water running through pipes. Did the housekeeper take a shower? Seems rather inappropriate. And strange. What if it's a reporter who somehow discovered I was here and broke into the house? Wouldn't be the first time those maniacs went to such extremes.

I pull up my phone to start texting Will, ready to ask him what's going on when the water suddenly shuts off, and a moment later, the door to the bathroom opens. Steam billows out, shrouding the room in a floral-scented fog, until my I snag on a pair of bright blue eyes. Before I can do anything other than blink, the woman belts out a scream, jumping high in the air, making the towel she was clutching against her chest fall to the floor in a wet heap.

For a moment, all I can do is stand here mesmerized. I haven't seen Faina since Will's wedding two years ago, and that night we did not hit it off. A blunder that was my own doing, but now as I take in her long, wet hair, glowing, smooth skin, and out-of-this-world stunning curves, I can't drag my eyes away even as I tell myself I have to.

*Faina. Holy hell. What is she doing here?*

Ava's sister never thought highly of me, though I've *always* had a thing for her. Ever since she let me cheat off her math test in our sophomore year of high school while pretending not to notice I was and then smiled and winked at me after.

"Dex?!" she shrieks, flying forward and snatching her towel off the floor and unfortunately wrapping it back around her body, though the sight of her in a towel is still pretty damn sexy. The loaded pistol pressing against the zipper of my trousers won't be going anywhere anytime soon with her like this. "What are you doing here?"

"Me?" I point to my chest, annoyed she's in my special hideaway when all I wanted was peace and solitude. Even if she is a literal wet dream come to life. "I'm staying here for the week. What are *you* doing here?" I turn that finger on her.

"You're not spending the week here. I am! I have nowhere else to go." She looks as though she's ready to skin me alive as her cheeks flush with fury and her pretty eyes narrow into tiny slits of hate. "I spoke to Ava just last night, and she told me the place was going to be empty."

Feeling the need to one-up her, I take a deliberate step forward, getting right up in her face. Feisty little minx doesn't back off even an inch. It's certainly not helping my situation below with her being fiery like this.

"Well, I spoke to Will yesterday afternoon, and *he* told *me* this place was all mine for the week. I just flew for more than fifteen hours, and I can tell you, I am not leaving." Frankly, I don't care what sort of misinformation her sister gave her. I realize Will feels like rubbish and is laid up in bed, so he and Ava likely didn't talk to each other about their rental. But there is no way in fucking hell I'm leaving now that I'm here.

If one of us is to leave, it's her.

An aggravated noise clears her throat. "No. No way. I got here first. I'm unpacked. I baked freaking cookies."

"Goodie gumdrops for you, love. Gold star for effort." Sarcasm drips from my tongue, enraging her. "I don't care if you've made a bloody five-course meal. I'm not leaving."

"You're such a bastard," she cries, shifting and tucking the top of her towel in tighter. "I see that hasn't changed. If you're looking for a new bed to make a sex tape in, you've come to the wrong place. Now leave. Fly back to whatever celebrity tabloid you crawled out of."

The disdain in her voice sets me off. I don't even know why. Maybe because I *have* been traveling for over fifteen hours and didn't sleep much on the plane. Maybe it's because I haven't slept much in the weeks prior to that. Maybe it's because no one fucking believes me that I didn't cheat and that my ex is the monster and not me.

Whatever it is, it has me lashing out. "You don't have to worry about me wanting to film a sex tape, princess. We're the only two people here, and I just got a good look at what you're hiding beneath that towel." The moment the words flee my lips, I instantly regret them. "Fuck," I hiss, wincing at her hurt expression that she quickly tries to hide with vitriol. I scrub my hand up and down my face, my voice and posture softening. "Listen, I'm sorry. I shouldn't have said that, and frankly, I didn't mean it. It's been a very long day and a very long couple of weeks. All of that bullshit is why I'm here hiding out."

"I'm not leaving," she grits out through clenched teeth. "I don't care about your celebrity woes. Some of us have real problems we have to figure out, and there's only one bed. Newsflash: We're not sharing it. So grab your bag and go find somewhere else to hide out."

My head pounds, and part of me wonders if it's worth the headache she's giving me. She hates me, and she has every right to after what I said about her at Will's wedding and then again just now. Maybe I should go and see if I can find another place nearby to stay. At least for tonight. Then I'll have to figure something else out. I don't own a home in the States anymore. My parents had one in LA that they sold after I completed boarding school there. My mum preferred London, and I couldn't blame her for it.

Faina is clearly not going anywhere, and I'm not sure how much fight I left in me. It seems I've reached my breaking point.

With a grunt, I turn and head for the door. Only something she said hits me, and I plant my hands into the frame, my back still to her. "Why don't you have anywhere else to go?" I ask gently, even with her mocking my life as celebrity problems.

She makes a pained noise in the back of her throat that has me turning to look over my shoulder. Grief seems to take over, and suddenly her tough-girl routine withers and dies before me.

"Not that it's any of your business, but I broke up with my boyfriend, and in doing so, I lost my job. They're fumigating my apartment in Boston this week, and I was going to be staying with him until I discovered his mistress. Something you clearly know all about."

I hold her gaze, ignoring the barb. "I'm sorry. That's rough."

She clears her throat and shifts her stance, obviously not having expected that response from me. Or my genuine sympathy for her.

"Thank you," she utters reluctantly.

"She wasn't my mistress," I state, though I don't know why I feel the need to defend myself. Maybe so she understands I'm actually in the same boat she is.

She's silent, watching me cautiously, so I continue.

"That video was taken from a threesome my ex orchestrated months ago. It was her idea. She picked the woman. She participated fully. Just not on video. Two weeks ago, I caught her screwing a stranger in our bed when she thought I was out of town. I broke his nose and got arrested for it because the prick pressed charges. Then when I ended it with her and sacked her as my PR manager, she retaliated. That's what you're seeing in the tabloids. That I cheated and then was a hothead who broke her new man's nose."

"Oh."

"Yeah. Oh." Suddenly I'm cheesed off all over again. "So you're not the only one with real-life problems. While I may be a celebrity, my music is my life, and she's fucked with that. I can't even leave my flat without being stalked and hounded by the world which hates me for something I didn't do. Now I have to try to find somewhere else to hide out." I storm out of the room, slamming the door behind me.

What the hell am I going to do now?

## Chapter Two

Faina

DEX'S WORDS sit heavy on my chest, and I don't like how they make me feel. Guilty. Guilty when I shouldn't be. He's an asshole. I hadn't seen him since high school, where I'd always harbored a ridiculous crush on him. I wasn't alone in that. Every girl did. He was tall and gorgeous and broody, and carried that rock star mystique about him even back then.

Then I overheard him at Ava's wedding talking to Will shortly before the ceremony. He referred to me as a beastly, snotty little princess who he'd have to suffer through during the ceremony and reception.

It hurt. Actually, it broke my heart a bit because I never knew he didn't like me, and high school crushes are the types of crushes that stick with you. All I had done was complain about how hot it was in the church in my dress, and then he said that. His girlfriend—who later became his cheating fiancée—laughed, and he smiled at her for it.

Even today, he's still calling me princess.

So yeah, Dex is an asshole. I shouldn't feel bad about staying here and kicking him out.

But as I get dressed—trying not to blush or think about the fact that he saw me naked—I can't stop thinking about it. About his situation and how closely it mimics my own, though thankfully I was only embarrassed in front of a hundred and fifty people while his trash has been dragged across the world.

I spend an extra few minutes pacing around the bedroom, and with a room this size, there's a lot of ground to cover. When I can't delay it another second and curiosity takes a firmer hold, I creep to the door, open it as quietly as I can, and listen.

I didn't hear the front door slam earlier, and with a hiss of a curse coming from the great room below, I know he's still here. While part of me expected him to already be gone, I suppose I'm not surprised he isn't.

Where else could he have gone?

My plan for today was to drink spiked Christmas drinks and eat my weight in chocolate and sugar cookies while depressing myself further by watching sappy holiday movies. In short, it was set to be a magnificent pity party, and if he's here, I can't do that. Can I? Would he want to join?

A weird twinge hits me, and I quickly brush it away as I pad down the stairs, awkwardness creeping in at how we left things. He's sitting at the counter in the kitchen, drinking a cup of coffee and helping himself to my cookies as he scowls at his laptop screen, and for a moment I watch him unob-served. Even sitting in the chair, he's much taller than me, with broad shoulders and a trim waist. The sleeves of his navy-blue sweater are pushed up to his elbows, showcasing his muscular forearms covered in colorful tattoos. His longish on top, sandy-blond hair is a disheveled mess, brushed back from his face as if he's been running his hands through it. A few days' worth of stubble lines his angled jaw, and when he mutters a slew of curses to himself, a dimple sinks into his cheek.

No doubt, Dex Chapman is a gorgeous man. Even for an asshole.

The floor creaks beneath my feet, and his green eyes sling-shot over to me. *Busted.* I push away from the wall and saunter unbothered into the kitchen. I help myself to a cup of coffee and then spin, leaning back against the island so I can face him as I hold the warm porcelain between my hands.

"More problems?" I quip, doing my best to maintain my sharp edge.

He grunts and takes a sip of his coffee. "There's nothing available nearby."

I'm not surprised by that. It's Christmas week. Hell, I couldn't even find a room to stay in last night in Boston. I ended up settling for a red-eye flight to Denver before taking a five a.m. jumper to Jackson, only to discover there were no rental cars available. I had to Uber here and then pay a fortune for grocery delivery.

I open my mouth to say something awful like, *It sucks to be you,* when my phone rings on the counter beside him where it's plugged into the wall. He snatches it up before I can get to it and then holds it up for me to see.

"Is this the bloke who broke your heart and had you fleeing to the middle of nowhere?" he taunts, wiggling the device back and forth.

The screen reads Brooks, and I sigh. It's the third time he's tried calling, though what he could possibly have to say to me, I have no idea. "Just hit ignore."

Only I should have known better because Dex gives me a shit-eating grin and then swipes his finger across the screen.

"Princess's phone," he answers.

I squawk, shooting forward like someone just hit my ass with a cattle prod. As I leap for him, my hip slams painfully into the side of the counter making me yelp, and nearly spill my coffee all over me. Unfortunately, it gives him enough time to jump out of his chair and move away from me.

"Give me the phone," I snap in a hushed murmur, not wanting Brooks to hear me. I set my mug down and glare furiously at him.

He shakes his head, his green eyes taunting. With a devious lick of his lips, he turns the phone to face me and then makes me watch as he puts it on speaker, all the while he continues to inch away from me toward the living room.

I give chase, leaving the kitchen and following him into the huge family room, only I take the other way around the sofa to cage him in a bit.

"Who the hell is this?!" Brooks yells, and I make a move, swiveling around the ottoman he just put between us and capturing his waist since he didn't even try to evade me. The jerk wanted me to catch him.

I jump up for the phone, and Dex smirks at me, holding the device high over his head and way out of my reach. His green eyes blaze into mine, that smirk curling up into a crooked grin. He makes a tsking noise at me, angling down until we're practically nose to nose, and then says with a mocking laugh, "Who am I? I'm the man currently with your ex-girl."

My eyes round, and I jump on him, making him oomph from the impact and stagger back a step. He stares down at me in shock as I practically climb up his chest to grab my phone, using his shoulders for leverage and wrapping my legs around his waist.

Dex belts out a laugh, his free arm banding tightly around me, refusing to let me move up higher to get to my phone even as he slams into the wall and then spins, walking us back toward the Christmas tree on the other side of the room.

"Where's Faina? Put her on the phone!"

"Not gonna happen, mate. I'm having far too much fun

with her right now." He smiles deviously at me, my face inches from his once more, his green eyes glowing.

"Who the fuck are you? Where is Faina? I need to talk to her right now. Put her on the fucking phone!"

"Give me the phone," I mouth, and Dex shakes his head, squeezing me tighter as I attempt to spring up and grab the phone. He has me locked against his chest now, my boobs squished and pushed up practically to my chin. I can't go up, and I can't go down. I'm trapped against a brick wall of muscle that smells irritatingly sexy and spicy and dangerous, like leather, musk, and fire.

"Oh, princess. It may have been years, but you should still know me better than that," he whispers, his warm breath fanning across my lips before he speaks louder toward the phone. "Brooks, I have to tell you, you gave up one hell of a feisty woman. In fact, she's climbing all over me as we speak. How daft are you to let this minx go? Have you seen what she looks like naked? Bad move, mate. Bad move."

"Oh, my God! I can't—"

Without warning, Dex's mouth slips to my neck and blows a raspberry, cutting off my words and making a high-pitched squeal tear from my lungs instead.

"Yeah. That's it. You love it when I put my mouth on you like that."

"Dex!" Only now I'm laughing too hard to speak as the hand crushing my ribs starts tickling me. "Ah! Stop! I'm ticklish there!" I'm laughing so hard I can hardly catch my breath as my legs flail and my arms push against his chest, trying to free myself.

"Oh, I know, princess, but I love when you scream my name like that. It makes me so hard. Come on. You can take it. Just a bit more. Give it to me just like that."

Brooks lets out a roar, and for a second, with Dex tickling me like this, I almost forgot my mission. Dex bellows out a yell as I sink my teeth into his shoulder. His grip slackens, and I use his pain and surprise to scoot up higher, shoving my boobs in his face along the way, but sacrifices must be made. Only as I reach for the phone and smother him with my chest, he's not only blind, but my movement and weight throw him off balance, and he trips over the foot of a chair.

A scream lurches from my lungs as we both go tumbling down to the floor in a heavy, hard heap, just narrowly missing the Christmas tree by inches.

An oomph careens from both of us, and my phone goes flying out of his hand and skidding across the floor where it smacks into the stone hearth. Dex is flat out on his back with me on top of him since he graciously broke my fall with his large body. He groans so I know he's not dead, but then I hear Brooks still yelling through my phone, and I move to climb off Dex to hit the end button once and for all when I feel something hard dig into my hip and freeze.

Dex freezes too as I lift my head up and peer down at him. "Is that?"

His eyes are shut and he's breathing hard, but he's smiling like a fool. "A pencil in my pocket? No. I'm just very happy to see you."

"What?" I snap, and his eyes slash open, twin emeralds nearly eclipsed by fat, round, black pupils.

He laughs at my appalled expression. "You were climbing me like a tree and wrapped around me like a monkey, princess. I told you it made me hard. I wasn't kidding. You may not have been aware that your pussy was grinding on my dick and that your tits were rubbing all over my chest and face, but I sure as hell was."

I flush like a fireball as heat shoots across my skin. Unexpectedly, my core clenches and my nipples harden, and that only feeds my embarrassment because I can't be sure he isn't aware of that last one. In fact, I think if the twist of his lips and the dark flare in his eyes are anything to go by, he is.

Shit.

I press my hands into the floor and push myself up, crawling off him while doing my best not to touch him or press more of my body against his—not so easily done from this position. I go for my phone, only Dex is quick and grasps my foot, sliding me back as he dives for it, snatching it and holding it up victoriously.

A shrill growl of frustration blows past my lips as he picks it up and then chirps, "Bye, Brooks. Don't call her again. It's my turn with her now." He hits the red button, disconnecting the call.

Foolishly he hands me my phone, and I'm tempted to bludgeon him with it. As it is, I shake it at him threateningly. "I can't believe you did that. You had no right."

"Were you interested in getting back together with him? Is all this, "I have no place to go and I'm hiding out in my sister's rental cabin" just a ploy to make lover boy come and chase after you?"

He sits up, leaning against the stone side of the fireplace, his long legs extending out as he casually adjusts his clothes. Meanwhile, I'm flat out on my stomach, my damp hair like a blonde curtain over my face. Bastard. I flip over and sit up, swooshing my hair out of my eyes and glaring at him.

"No," I seethe. "I'm not getting back together with him, and I don't want him to chase after me. He cheated, and as far as I'm concerned, we're over."

He tilts his head, giving me a crooked grin that makes his dimples pop and his green eyes sparkle. "Then what harm is there in torturing the chap a bit? He clearly has it coming, and now he's jealous, stewing in his own juices."

I fall back onto the carpet, staring up at the tall ceiling and dark wood beams. Inhaling a deep breath, I release it slowly as tears prickle my eyes. "I suppose you're right. I should make him suffer. I should seek revenge on him for what he did to me. He embarrassed me. Last night we were at our office holiday party. A hundred and fifty colleagues and clients, and his affair was broadcast to all of them." I turn away, my face scrunching up. Thinking about him gives me a hangover that has nothing to do with that massive martini I drank half of.

Dex is silent and still as he listens, and that only spurs me on.

"He told me he loved me. We'd only been dating a month when he said it. I thought I had everything. I had a guy who loved me. I had the best job, one I loved doing and was very good at. I loved the people I worked with. I felt important and smart and successful and fucking loved. He stripped all that from me in the blink of an eye." A tear rolls down my cheek and then into my hair. "He called me horrible and boring, and everyone heard it." I hiccup out a sob.

"What do you mean by that? Horrible and boring how?"

Fury and humiliation tear through me. "He told the woman he was screwing he thought I was horrible in bed. That I was so bland and unadventurous I even made vanilla bored with me. Or something like that. The only reason he didn't want to end it with me was because I'm good at my job and he didn't want to lose me in his firm. He used me and cheated on me without an ounce of remorse, and I didn't even know that's the type of man he is."

I sit up and wipe at my face, meeting Dex's serious expression. "How can I go back to Boston? Those clients…" I trail off, shaking my head. "They're big players, and they heard *everything* he said. What happened will be all over the city. He humiliated me, and that sort of thing follows you. It'll always be whispered about behind my back no matter where I go or what I do."

"Well, now he thinks you're having hot, wild sex. That show we just put on sounded anything but horrible or boring."

I shrug. "I suppose, but it certainly wasn't real, and it doesn't help me with my job or those people."

"I look like an asshole to the world." He pans a hand out toward me. "You proved that earlier. No one believes me. It's one thing for musicians to fuck groupies—hell, it's expected of us, revered even as part of our bad boy mystique—but the world thinks you're a slimy piece of shit when you cheat and a total creeper when you make a sex tape. Plus, I was arrested for assault. My endorsements are threatening to pull out. My label is furious, and I know they're talking about doing the same. The truth is, I knew something wasn't quite right between us. She kept pushing for marriage, and something inside me just couldn't pull the trigger. She fucked around, ruined my name, and came out looking like the sad victim in all of this. The only clever thing I ever did with her was not give her access to my money, which she tried for several times over. That should have been a red flag."

"He spent dozens of late nights 'working' on the party with her." I put air quotes around the word. "She was the event coordinator. He'd come over sometimes after and shower, and I didn't even put it together." I shake my head, staring down at my hands in my lap. "So stupid. And so awful. Sometimes we'd have sex after his shower… after he was with her that same night."

"My ex is the reason I said what I said to Will about you on his wedding day."

My eyes shoot up to his. "She is?"

He shrugs, looking sheepish. "She was jealous of you. You walked in looking like a princess in your pale pink gown, and I stared for a few seconds longer than I likely should have. She caught me and was angry, and I told her I thought you were a cow."

"A cow?" My eyes grow bigger than the moon. "Is that because I'm…" I trail off, unable to say the word, but gesture to my breasts, hips, and thighs so he gets my meaning all the same.

Horror strikes his features. "Fuck no. And don't you dare say or think anything of the sort. Your curves are fucking sexy, Faina. You just felt the proof of that, so don't say it isn't true."

He chuckles and gives me another shrug. "She didn't buy that excuse, but then I heard you complain about it being hot in the church, which it was, and then later, when Will asked me about you in front of her, I had to say something disparaging. Then I spent the rest of the night ignoring you. It was a shitty thing to do, and I'm sorry. I regretted it the rest of the evening and well beyond. You had every right to hate me for it. You were always sweet and kind to me when we were in school, and I was anything but to you that evening."

"She's a bitch."

He chuckles. "Thank you. Agreed." He pulls his knees up and rests his forearms on them. "And your ex is a wanker and a daft fool. I wasn't lying when I said that to him."

"Thank you. I'm sorry she's making you look bad while getting away with what she did to you."

"Thank you. I'm sorry he embarrassed you publicly and ruined a job and career you love. If I had known all that he'd done prior to that phone call, he would have gotten a lot more from me on that. He never should have spoken badly about…"

"About how boring I evidently am in bed?"

He gives me a diffident smile. "Yeah. That."

I bluster out a sound, playing self-consciously with the sleeve of my sweater even as I nod in gratitude. We both have it pretty rough right now.

"The couch doesn't look so bad," I murmur under my breath, wondering if I'm crazy for even suggesting this.

"Oh? You're willing to sleep on the sofa. That's quite generous of you."

I snort, rolling my eyes at him. "Fat chance of that. *You're* the one without options on places to stay."

"The king bed looked accommodating. I have no doubt it could fit both of us perfectly."

I squint at him. "Not a chance in hell."

"Oh, come now. I'd be happy to help you prove your ex wrong."

I glare at that, even as my insides flutter. I know he doesn't mean it. "It's the couch or nothing for you."

He tilts his head, scrutinizing me. "Are you genuinely offering for me to stay then? As in we'll spend the holidays here? Together?"

Am I? "Horrible idea?"

He rubs a finger along his bottom lip, his green eyes dancing with a mischievous glint. "Not as horrible as the one I'm having."

# Chapter Three

Dex

"WHY DO I get the feeling I'm going to regret offering for you to stay?" Faina questions, wariness lining her features.

She's going to think I'm mad. But the truth is, I've had an ace of an idea, and it stemmed from her. She used the word revenge, and while that sounds brilliant to me, as I'd love nothing more than to make Elsie suffer for all she's done, I think I might have a better idea.

Certainly, a more beneficial one for both of us.

I sit up, inching closer to her, my eyes all over her face, and with that, there is no denying just how gorgeous she is. Long, blonde hair, big, bright blue eyes, and full, naturally pink lips. She's petite, more than a foot shorter than me, with an edible, curvy body. Yeah, her ex is a real tosser for giving her up. The way she looks—fuck, the way she felt when she was all over me.

It was my teenage dream come to life. I wanked my cock to her plenty of times when we were kids. No way she's boring in bed. Timid maybe. She's always been that.

But perhaps she just needs the right coach to guide her along. To make her feel beautiful, sexy, and desirable. To peel her out of her shell piece by piece.

Then again, that might be the wrong track to take this. I don't know Faina well, at least not anymore, but I do know she's the commitment, relationship type, and not the fun-only type. As of forever, the latter is the only type I'm interested in. Plus, she's been through it, and I won't take advantage of that. Despite my current reputation, I've never been the bad guy in any woman's story, and I'm not about to change that.

Especially when reversing my image is the name of the game I'd like to play with her.

I switch tactics.

"Your ex deserves to have what he gave up rubbed in his face, and I need to fix my image and my career. I'm thinking this could be an advantageous week for both of us."

She stares at me, long and hard, and then finally shakes her head. "I don't understand."

"Well, originally I was going to offer you my sexual services, be something of a guru or coach, but I figured you'd kick me in the bollocks for that."

And didn't I *just* say I wasn't going to try and fuck this woman? Thankfully her look of revulsion settles my eager dick down. You'd think my man hadn't been in a pussy in decades the way he responds to her.

"You'd be correct." She quirks an unamused eyebrow at me, and I press on.

"Here's my thought. We take cute photographs with sweet as spun sugar captions and post them on our social media. It'll drive your ex mad while making the world forget about Elsie and instead focus on the lovely princess I'm currently with. Plus, you're... normal." I gesticulate toward her, running my hand up and down. "Wholesome. My best mate's sister-in-law. It doesn't have to look as though we're a couple. In fact, it's likely better if it doesn't so people don't think I'm a man whore. Just... you know... spending time with a friend."

She stares skeptically at me. "Why on earth would I want the world to think I'm here with you, as a friend or otherwise?"

"Women love that. Being seen with someone famous."

She shakes her head. "Not me. You realize this idea benefits you far more than it does me, right?"

"That's why I thought the sex lessons might be fun and even things out a bit, but I retract that. Besides, you mentioned how you're worried about your marketing and PR reputation. If you're photographed with me and we're able to pull this off the way I believe we will, your name will be out there, and I'd bet a thousand quid the job offers start rolling in for you. I'll also put in a good word for you anywhere you interview."

"Still sounds like you need me in this way more than I need you."

"Then consider it doing a favor for your beloved brother-in-law's best man."

She rolls her eyes, but I can see she's caving. "I'm not kissing you," she tells me in no uncertain terms.

"Fantastic. I bet you kiss like a snake."

Her eyebrows shoot up. "A snake? You've kissed a lot of those to know by comparison?"

A laugh tickles my lips. "Actually, I have. My ex, for starters." I'm having way too much fun with her. "All tongue and no lips? I can tell just by looking at you that that's how you kiss."

"What sort of self-respecting rock star gets cheated on? I can tell by looking at you that you're lazy in bed."

Ouch. "Should I throw that back at you?"

"Nope. I'm already covered in that dirt and don't need it rubbed in my face again."

I drop forward, sitting like a small child and propping my

forearms on the floor so I'm that much closer to her. "Fine then. But here we are. Two people who have been cheated on with the opportunity to help the other out. What do you say? Be my princess for the week? Grant me this Christmas wish. I'm desperate."

"So, I see. If I agree to take stupid pictures with your ugly mug to get you out of social media and unpopular opinion prison, we are not getting naked."

"Again, you mean. Since you already did that with me today."

And what is *wrong* with me? It's like I can't help myself. Two and a half years of being with the same woman, and it's as if now that I'm a free man, my brain is short-circuiting. Reminding me that there are other—possibly far more lovely—fish in the sea for me to entertain myself with. Only I can't entertain myself with this particular fish.

She is an endangered species where I'm concerned.

"Forget it," she declares, exasperated. "Deal's off."

"No." I fly forward and tackle her back to the floor until I have her pinned beneath me. "I'm sorry. I'll behave. Just do this with me, princess. Please."

"You're literally on top of me and you want me to do this with you?"

I laugh. "That's a fantastic dirty joke, my pretty minx, and though a large part of me"—I wink at her—"is dying to answer in the affirmative, I'll behave like a good lad and keep my fingers, mouth, and cock to myself. Even if that won't benefit you at all."

She rolls her eyes and then pushes against me. "Off. I can't imagine there's any part of you, large or small, that I'd benefit from. I'll agree because I think you might have a point in letting me exploit your celebrity name, and frankly, I don't have a lot of options otherwise. You can start by buying me breakfast. I was going to only eat sugar and only drink alcohol, but I think my stomach is starting to require more."

"I have a car," I offer.

"You do?"

I blink at her. "Yes. Why so stunned? It was Will's rental he set up that I took over."

She heaves a sigh as I shift off her. "I couldn't find a car to rent."

I give her my most charming yet devilish grin. "Well, then it's lucky your new temporary lover comes equipped... with a car. And money." I jump up to my feet and grasp her hand, forcing her to do the same. "Come on. Let's go spend some of it. I've heard the shops in this town are very western, whatever that means, but I'm positive we can make that work for us as long as I don't have to wear a cowboy hat or boots." I twirl her around in a circle, making her laugh before I haul her into my chest and then dip her back. "A true Englishman should never wear either." I flip her upright and then twist her once more toward the door.

She's so small I can practically do whatever I want with her. A thought that instantly heats my blood, but I put all of that on the back burner as we bundle up and climb into my rental Range Rover. And yes, I absolutely get in on the right side of the car, only for her to correct me that I'm required on the left.

I start to pull out of the driveway, only the car begins to skid, and I slam on the breaks, causing the rear of the car to fishtail slightly.

"Fuck," I hiss. "Have you ever driven in this white shit?"

She's biting her lip, trying hard not to laugh. "I live in Boston."

"And it snows there?" I question. "I've been there three times, but each of those times was playing concerts and always in the summer. It never snowed in LA, and it rarely snows in London and never like this. I can already tell you, I'm not a fan."

"I'm very used to driving in the snow," she promises.

"Swap places with me. I'm not sure I feel comfortable with you driving on the right side of the road and in the snow."

I grip the wheel, feeling the need to validate my manhood with her now that we're not moving. "For the record, I could drive us if I had to. I drove when we were teenagers on the right side of the road."

She's smirking at me. My lovely princess is smirking at me. It makes me want to kiss that mocking thing straight off her lips. I don't think she's boring. I saw her in action today. When properly motivated, she's a wildfire.

"I remember." She pats my arm like I'm a small child. "Now hop out and try not to slip on all that white stuff we Americans call snow."

I make an annoyed, huffy boy noise, but who am I kidding? I'll kill us both if I try to drive.

"You don't own the snow, American. I know you think you own everything, but you don't. Try venturing to Europe. Your mountains are small and young in comparison."

"That's what makes us so desirable," she tells me without a hint of sarcasm, and I'm starting to like her. In a purely platonic way, of course. But she's fun. A bit barmy, but that only adds to her charm.

We do the switch, but before she can drive us away, I say, "First a selfie." I pull out my mobile and then drag her by the shoulder over to me until our heads are pressed together over the center console. "Smile, princess, and make it look believable."

I hold the phone up and over us, angling it just right, and then I snap a picture of our smiling faces capped by snow hats. Righting myself, I stare at the picture for a moment. At just how good we look together. At how natural it seems in that captured moment when it's anything but.

I go into my Instagram and set up the picture when I falter. "What do I write?"

She thinks about this as she starts to drive us like a pro

toward town. Finally, she suggests, "Braving the snow and the cold in the name of brunch with an old friend."

I blink at my phone as I start to type that in. "That's it?"

"It'll make them wonder. Always leave them questioning and wanting more. Don't tag me, and definitely don't geolocate yourself. The questions and comments will start, and they'll bring a lot of buzz to your post."

I do as she says and then slide my phone back into my trousers pocket. "You're good at this. But why am I not tagging you?"

She throws me a sideways grin before returning to the road. "Because Brooks will already be checking into you, so that side of this is handled. He knows my brother-in-law is friends with you and I believe I yelled out your name as you so artfully commented. But having me be a woman of mystery, a woman you want to be photographed with but don't want to be known by name, will bolster this up for you and create a buzz that's not entangled in your current issue."

"I should hire you to be my new PR manager," I quip, but my joke falls heavy with a thud between us as a frown mars her lips, and I let it die there. We drive the rest of the way to a brunch place I pull up on my phone in relative silence and I have no way to fill it. This wasn't what I was searching for when I got on the plane yesterday, but somehow, it's so much better than being alone or festering in my wounds.

Yet something is sticking with me. Something I can't quite place.

It isn't until we park on the quaint western-style street with its upscale yet small-town feel that I realize I'm having fun with her. And I can't remember the last time I had that. Not with Elise. Not in my day-to-day life. I've been writing and creating music on an endless cycle where it became more work than love or passion. Touring that consisted of endless months on the road and longer than long days. And then back in the studio for the next round.

A joyful flutter hits my belly and swooshes through my blood, making my muscles jump and my bones content.

When was the last time I took a break? When was the last time I stopped to simply go out for brunch?

Not even when Mum was alive did I do this with her—a regret I'll now carry to my grave. I have a week of total freedom with a woman who isn't the least bit interested in me for much of anything. I can relax. I can be myself. I don't have to try and impress her.

It's bloody fantastic.

Tossing on my ball cap that I picked up in the airport and my aviators, I hop out of the SUV and onto the quaint street, taking in the scene around me. "Motherfuck is that an arch made out of horns?"

Faina stares down the street toward the green area. "I believe they're antlers."

"Is there a difference?"

She shrugs. "No clue, but it's kind of creepy and cool all at once. Let's eat. I'm starving." I join her on the sidewalk, and she peers up at me. More than a head shorter than I am, she comes up to my shoulder. "Also, you might want to cool it with the British accent. It'll do nothing but call attention to you."

I snort. "Sure. Yeah. I can talk like an American. Yeee-hah!" I bark out, doing my best American accent that has her cracking up.

"That was horrible."

I smile, staring down at her, taking in the different shades of blue in her eyes and the way the cold turns her cheeks and the tip of her nose pink. "Thank you for letting me stay."

"You're welcome. Thankfully you come with a car and money, as you said, so it'll work out. It might be a bit strange and certainly awkward, but what the hell? We'll drink and cook and hang out, and I even heard there are hot springs nearby."

"Hot springs?" I like the sound of that. "Will mentioned a hot tub in the garden."

"That sounds—" Her voice cuts off as her phone pings. She pulls it out, checks it, and then frowns. "Well, Brooks saw your post."

"And?" My eyebrows shoot up as I try to angle myself to see her screen.

She shakes her head, chewing miserably on her bottom lip. "Let's go in." Without waiting on me, she walks into the restaurant. "Two, please. Somewhere in the back, if you can," she says to the hostess.

I linger back a few steps until she's seated, and then I join her, keeping my head ducked down, though no one here is paying much attention to me. It's a dream. I want to press her about the text, but I don't think she'd consider me a friend yet, and frankly, I'm not sure how far I can push her. We peruse the menu, but I can tell her mind is still on whatever her twat of an ex said.

"Can I start you with some coffee while you're going over the me— Oh my gosh! You're Dex Chapman, aren't you?"

Bollocks. Here we go.

"You're a jerk," the waitress exclaims, growing angry on behalf of a woman she doesn't know or perhaps on behalf of all womankind.

"He's not," Faina defends, and I can't stop my shocked expression. Faina signals the waitress to come closer, as if she's about to tell her a secret. "He never cheated. His ex did, and then when he broke up with her because of it, she set him up with an old video and a bunch of lies. Trust me, he's the one who's been wronged, but he's a man and a rock star, right? No one believes him, and everyone believes her because that's how our world works."

The waitress blinks at Faina, and then her head twists in my direction, suddenly appraising me with sympathy like I'm a lost dog in need of saving.

"Oh, you poor thing. That's so awful that she did that to you. I'm so sorry I called you a jerk."

"No bother," I say because, frankly, I'm used to it already.

"As you can imagine, things have been tough," Faina continues, laying it on a bit thick. "Listen, he'll sign anything you want as long as you don't let on that we're here." Faina blinks prettily at the waitress, who is now one hundred percent Team Dex. If Faina has this sort of power and charm, all jokes aside, I might need to hire her after all. "We're trying for a quiet getaway and heard you have the best brunch in town. Dex is a real sucker for brunch. And handsomely tipping agreeable waitresses. Aren't you, buddy?"

*Buddy?* "Um. Yeah. Sure." Then I think better of it. "I am actually. My lovely friend here enjoys baking, but we both prefer to brunch out. Since we're here for the week, we'd love to be able to return." I let the full meaning of my words rest on her shoulder, and she quickly starts nodding.

"Of course! I won't say anything."

She's all of seventeen, so I'm not sure how much I believe her.

"This is my family's place," she tells us conspiratorially. "If you put in a good review and possibly mention how amazing the food was at the end of your week, I won't say a word to anyone. I'm trying to save up for college," she tacks on, and I nearly chuckle.

"If you keep that promise, I will help with those savings, and we'll be sure to make a special post about your family's restaurant."

Her eyes light up like the Christmas trees lining the square. "I promise."

"Fantastic. Are you ready to order?" I ask Faina, gesturing in her direction. She orders a cheese omelet with wheat toast. That's it. And though I'm loathsome to use the word, it's a boring order. Perhaps she does need a bit of an… awakening. I decide here and now to do that for her. She's already helping

29

me, and she's right, there isn't much benefit for her in that. I'll help her discover the woman I know she is on the inside. I've seen glimpses, and those glimpses are enough to tell me that she's in there.

Just hiding.

Maybe if she lets go a little, the sex will naturally follow— even if it's not with me.

"I'll have the Spanish omelet with sourdough toast, strawberry jam, sausage, and bacon, please. And coffee. For both of us."

"You got it."

The waitress skips off, gleeful as one of Santa's elves.

"No tea? You're English. So very, *very* English."

I ignore Faina's not-so-thinly veiled jab. "I only drink tea in the afternoon. Coffee in the morning." And because I have issues keeping my mouth shut and my curiosity at bay, I ask her, "What did the git say in his text, and can I find a new way to torture him for it?"

I'm not actually jesting about that. I'd love to ruin him for hurting her. She's this tiny, sweet little thing who I can't help but want to take care of and protect. The way she's done for me this morning.

She purses her lips and stares out into the restaurant I have my back to. That's another thing she did for me. She sat in the position to face out, giving me more privacy. Considering how our morning started, it's more than I deserve from her. She could have already exploited me ten different ways, but she hasn't.

She's been kind and protective, and though trust in my world is hard to come by—even more so now after what my ex did—here I am trusting her and sharing a cabin and my holiday with her. I didn't even have to think about it. It just happened, and I never once questioned her intentions or motives.

Maybe because we grew up together and I know her sister

Ava as well as I do. A woman who married a billionaire for love and not money.

Faina seems just as loyal and guarding as her sister. A quality I both like and admire.

I wait her out, and once our coffee is delivered and we both add in our cream and sugar, she surprises the fuck out of me by asking, "Were you serious when you offered your bedroom knowledge and services to me?"

## Chapter Four

Faina

I ADMIT, the last thing I should be is vulnerable. But I'm fresh and raw and fucking hurt. It may seem pathetic, but him calling me shitty in bed zings worse than him cheating and I can't even explain why that is. Maybe because I suspect he wouldn't have cheated, if I was halfway decent in bed, and *that* pisses me off even more.

Because he should never have cheated, and I shouldn't feel bad about myself because he did, and I shouldn't allow him to control or manipulate my sense of self-worth.

But I am.

Or maybe it's more that I'm questioning the woman I've allowed myself to become. I felt no heat when I was with Brooks. I never had the urge to rip his clothes off and never had a moment where I struggled to keep my hands to myself. I liked him because he was smart and dependable, and we were good together.

A perfect social match.

That's it.

But Brooks texting me that Dex Chapman will grow bored of me in minutes and I'll come begging for Brooks to take me back hits me in all the worst places. I can't go back. And I don't want to be considered boring—in bed or otherwise. I don't want to be dull and allow the hottest, best moments of my life to pass me by because I'm too afraid to make the leap.

That's how I've been my entire life. Ava was the adventurous one, afraid of nothing, and I was the opposite, the quiet good girl, too cautious, practical, and afraid to make any waves.

Not anymore.

This is my wake-up call. And Dex is the perfect man for the job.

He's a rock star, and I'm a normal girl as he put it. He lives in London, and I live in Boston. He too is just getting out of a bad relationship, so he definitely won't be looking for another. And from what I saw of that video, the man *knows* what he's doing in the bedroom. Plus, my body has reacted more to Dex in the last three hours than it ever did to Brooks in the months we were dating.

I *need* to feel this. I need to explore it. I need to believe I am not the problem; I've just been with the wrong men.

Dex gives me a look that tells me he doesn't quite know how to answer. Finally, after he sucks down a hearty sip of coffee, he decides to give it to me straight. "Yes." Simple. Finite.

But there is a burning ember in the back of his green eyes that tells me he means it.

We have no chance at a future. No possibilities beyond this. It's sex and nothing else.

He knows it.

I know it.

I'm positive there's a part of my mind trying desperately to remind me why this is a bad idea, but I'm tired of listening to that part of me. Dex is the kind of reckless disaster that should have me running, but for the first time in my life, I don't want to run away. I want to run toward the chaos.

I want something incredible to remember when this is all over.

And I know he can give me that if I let him.

"Good. That's what I want," I tell him after our breakfast is set before us and the waitress leaves us again.

"What happened to all your, I won't kiss you and I won't touch you and I certainly won't share a bed with you?"

I shrug. "I changed my mind."

His eyes grow hard. "What did he say to you?"

I glance down. "That you'll grow bored of me, and I'll come crawling back to him."

"He's a prat, love. A slimy little weasel who wants to have his cake and eat it too. Men like him get off on bringing others—especially women—down to make themselves feel powerful and more important. He's not the reason you should fall into bed with someone."

I grit my teeth. "He's not," I snap. "I'm doing this for myself. I'm twenty-seven. I have a degree in public relations and a master's in business and marketing. I graduated top of my class from Ivy League schools, and I did so with full scholarships. I've worked for two top firms in Boston, both of which I was recruited to. I'm smart, but... I'm boring." The admission hurts, but it needs to come out if I'm going to do this. "I eat well, exercise daily, wear sensible heels, and I never ever spend too much money on anything. I date successful, well-positioned men and keep up on current events. I'm a snooze-fest." I shove my plate toward him. "Look, even my breakfast is boring."

He rubs a finger along his bottom lip. "I wasn't going to say anything, but yeah, it is."

"See?" I throw my hands up in the air. "I need this. I'm too young to live this life. I'm not saying I want to go out and get a tattoo or a piercing or blow all my savings on a purse.

I'm just saying I need to live a little before it's too late, and I think having some hot sex is a good way to start."

He falls back against the cushion of the booth and glares skeptically. "Do you know what you're asking for with me?"

I match his position. "You mean do I understand that I'm asking you to have no-string sex ed with me?"

He smirks. "Yes."

"One hundred percent. It's the perfect situation. We're not going to fall in love. This is one week of total madness that happened to throw us together. And I don't want to be her. The woman who gets cheated on and is told in front of too many people that the reason she was cheated on is because she's shitty in bed." I stare down at the Formica table. "I didn't feel much when I had sex with him. Not a lot of lust or excitement. He never made me crazy." I look up at Dex. "I want a man to make me feel crazy. I want to be so overcome with desire that I can't keep my hands to myself. I want to see sparks fucking fly."

Neither of us has touched our food. We're too busy locked in this standoff.

"You want a man to make you crazy? To make sparks fly?"

"It's more than that. I want to experience sex and know that I unequivocally own it along with the man who is brave enough to crawl into bed with me. I want to be wild and adventurous and unafraid. I want to be able to look back on my life one day and say, "I did that." I was that woman."

He emits a shaky chuckle, his face casting sideways out toward the restaurant and the people not paying us a whole lot of attention. While he's mulling my proposition over, I pick up my fork and reach across, jabbing his sausage and then bringing it to my lips to take a bite. He catches it, his lips quirking up into an amused grin. He snatches the fork from my hand and shoves the rest into his mouth, chewing and swallowing all the while staring at me.

"Princess, I can make sparks fly. I can make them dance

behind your eyes. I can take you out for a ride and twist you up until you're mine."

A smile lightens my face. "Those sound like song lyrics."

He smiles right back at me. "Maybe they'll turn out to be. You're sure? You're absolutely positive you want to start messing around? With me?"

"If you're in, I'm in."

His eyebrows bounce, and he munches on a piece of bacon. "Oh, I'm in. I was in the moment you dropped your towel. You've already felt how eager my dick is for you, and if you were to peer beneath the table, you'd see how much he's enjoying this conversation."

I gasp and move to look, but he reaches out, snatching my wrist, stopping me. His eyes are fierce in warning.

"You'll see plenty of him soon enough. But, love—"

"It's only this week," I say in no uncertain terms, cutting him off. "I know. I agree, so you don't have to worry. It'll just be fun. A lot of exploration. No feelings will be involved. We have this week, and it's us doing this thing where I help you and you help me, but that's it."

Something crosses his face but clears before I can tell what it is. "Agreed," he pushes out. "I have rules though." He starts cutting into his omelet, and I do the same with mine.

"Such as?" I ask as I fork a bite into my mouth.

"You let me lead. You do as I say without question unless it truly makes you uncomfortable. You trust that I won't hurt you or take you down a path I don't think you can handle."

I swallow my eggs, practically choking on them since my throat suddenly went dry. Washing them down with a large sip of coffee, I think about that. "That's an awful lot of trust for a man I hardly know."

"You know me. It's just been a while. Besides, you clearly trust me enough to ask me to be your sexual guru."

"Fine. Touché. Will you hurt me?"

His eyes grow impossibly dark, and his tongue swipes out,

gliding along his bottom lip. "Only in ways I know you'll love. Don't worry, princess. I vow to take good care of you."

Heat blooms on my cheeks, and I giggle lightly. "This is not where I thought my week would go."

His lips twitch. "Mine either, but I'd be lying if I said I wasn't looking forward to it now, whereas before I wasn't." I'm about to say it's the same for me when he cuts me off with, "I fucking want to eat you instead of these eggs."

"Dex!"

He laughs at my outrage. "You better start getting used to it." He winks at me, and I shake my head.

There is no denying him when he smiles at you like that. All green eyes and full lips and boyish dimples. Dex is too gorgeous to be real. He has the kind of face that makes your chest flutter and your insides squirm every time you look at him. He stops women in their tracks and makes them stare mindlessly. I assume he's used to it by now. He got famous quickly. Almost straight after high school, a label picked him up and turned him into a household name.

He's talented, and his music is amazing. But there's a lot to be said about the way his mouth curls around not just song lyrics but his dirty words and the resulting way my body responds. It makes me nervous. In both a good and a bad way. I'm going to have to let go of my inhibitions and lock down my heart if I'm going to keep up with him this week.

He sits forward and drops his forearms on the table, all playfulness gone. "We can't ever let Will know about this. He'd slaughter me. His wife is his greatest love, and you're not just her sister, but her twin. So I'm risking some shit here, but I already know the risk will be well worth the reward."

I roll my eyes derisively as I shift my eggs around on my plate. "I'm an adult, Dex, and I don't think Ava will care if you and I have a holiday fling. Hell, knowing her, she'd tell me to go for it."

His lips bounce. "Holiday fling? Is that what we're calling this?"

"It has a certain ring to it. It sounds merry and fun. It makes me want to wear a Santa hat and nothing else."

He laughs. "Thaaaat, I'd love to see. Oh, no wait." He gives me a dirty once-over. "Red. Lace. Possibly with a bow over your arse so I can unwrap you like a present." He groans. "Fuck, I'm getting too hard to be sitting here." He shifts, visibly adjusting himself, and my empty core clenches.

A flurry of butterflies takes flight in my stomach, and I nearly belt out a girlish giggle. Holy hell. I'm going to do this. I'm actually going to have a holiday fling with Dex Chapman. A dirty holiday fling from the sound of it.

Good thing I waxed before the party last night.

And now I do laugh because last night suddenly feels so far away, and all that negative energy I'd been swimming in has suddenly evaporated. I've taken control of my life. Of my situation. I may be jobless, but I can work that out. I always do.

But for the first time in my life, I'm throwing caution to the wind, and I'm *excited* for it.

"I don't have red lace or bows, but I did pack my naughtiest underwear."

"Is it Santa-approved naughty list naughty?" he questions, and when his dimples pop, I remind myself it's just one week and nothing more and to keep my high school crush where it is. In the past.

"Probably not to your rock star specifications."

"Hmmm." He contemplates this seriously. "Let's finish up. I'm having an idea for your first lesson."

## Chapter Five

Dex

MY DICK HAS NEVER BEEN SO hard in my life. And I'm not saying that to be crass. I'm simply stating biological facts, and though I'm trying to talk the anxious boy down, he's not listening. He was just propositioned by our high school crush for a week of sex lessons. He's eager. He's excited. He's ready to take the challenge by storm and start right here in the restaurant.

Which is why we need to get out of here. Now.

"Oh, are we going skiing?"

That pulls me up short. "Pardon?"

She starts cackling and then suddenly stops as well. "You don't ski, do you?"

"Um. No."

I get a big, sweet smile. "We could try. Ava does it and says it's the best."

Again. "Um. No."

"How can you be here"—she pans her hands around—"and not ski?"

"Simple. I didn't pick the location, the location picked me. I don't get on two wooden sticks and fly down a mountain made of snow. And before you get it in your pretty little head to question, no, I don't snowboard either. This is my first vacation in a million years, but I can tell you, I would have much preferred Will telling me he had rented a beach-front villa on some exotic island to the cold and snow."

"Christmas isn't Christmas if it's warm," she counters.

"Christmas is what you make it, love. Weather is of no consequence." I tilt my head. "Are you deliberately bating me or are you simply stalling?"

"Neither," she declares. "I love the snow and have always wanted to try skiing but never had an excuse." Her eyebrows bounce at me. "Think of how your fans will go crazy over a picture of you on skis for the first time. They'll swoon."

I grumble. "Your pussy better be bloody magic."

She laughs. "Didn't I just hire you to be my magician?"

"Your pussy magician I shall be. If we can ever pay the check."

She signals the waitress over, and I snicker.

My lovely princess is impatient. She's reactive. She's going to blossom beneath my touch, and then…

And then I've opened up her flower for other men to touch and appreciate.

My teeth unerringly clench, and my fists grip my fork and knife. I stare down at my plate and force myself to remember that long-term women are no longer part of my dating plan.

I can do sex with Faina. It'll give me something new to be haunted by, and her memory will be far sweeter than my ex's because she's being upfront about what she wants and doesn't want from me.

Which just so happens to perfectly coincide with what I'm after.

Sex. Nothing else.

Even as my winter princess starts chatting with our waitress while tossing the occasional sweet smile in my direction. She's out of my league. Far too good for me. She always has been. But this week... this week she's going to be mine.

And in the process... maybe we'll take each other's pain away.

I'm on guard for the entire world, but with her, I'm effortlessly me, and there's a lot to be said for that. Especially after the last two weeks, I've had. I pay the check and then take her hand since that's the game we're playing. I can only hope someone photographs us and posts it, and we look just the way I know we do.

Big, secret smiles and stolen glances and heat rising between us.

The ballcap is gone in favor of my beanie. It's too cold for anything else, and as we tuck into each other, marching down the sidewalk, fighting the frigid air, I draw her into the shop I had seen earlier that I thought might make things a bit of fun.

Only the moment we walk in, I'm reminded that we're in Wyoming and not New York City or LA. This women's only clothing shop is not sexy. It's a lot of heavy wool, thick frameless flannels, and large, stompy boots.

"Um. What are we doing in here?" Faina leans into me, whispering the words through the side of her mouth.

"I thought women's clothing would have sexy bits."

She laughs. "Do you not know what part of the country you're in?"

"I'm learning."

The saleswomen who remind me of my grandmum are staring at us with genuine curiosity. And while they appear kind and welcoming, I don't think this is the aesthetic I was going for.

But because I'm me, I say, "Sorry, I was searching for delicious pieces of confection I can strip off my friend here."

I can practically feel the heat rising off her skin as she gasps. "I can't believe you just said that!"

The women stare at us, and then one of them smiles in amusement. "If you're looking for that type of thing, the Four Seasons has a store." She blinks at me and then winks like we're in this together. "And a spa."

"Ah. Brilliant. Thank you!" I walk across the store and drop a hundred on the counter. "Merry Christmas."

"God bless!" they call after us, and then I'm dragging her to the car, both of us slamming doors to keep the cold out.

"Fuck the Four Seasons. We'll be snaked out of that drain faster than a London sewer."

She laughs at my choice of words. "Is that so?"

"Without a doubt. I'll have to order straight from the source with expedited shipping. Obviously."

"Obviously," she parrots. But her mocking lilt does something to me, and suddenly my hand scoops into her hair, and then I'm cupping the back of her neck and dragging her lips to mine. The way I've wanted to all day. Hell, the way I've wanted to since I first laid eyes on her when I was fifteen.

And it's so fucking good. So much better than I imagined it would be all these years.

The kiss is firm and solid, but *soft*. Like marshmallows in hot chocolate melting into gooey, sticky sweetness you can't get enough of.

She hums against me, making my toes curl in my boots, and I react by finding the roots of her hair and gripping them for dear life. Her lips… I sigh against them and then twist my head the other way, seeking a new angle, seeking more. She's so deliciously malleable as I maneuver her every way I want. Our tongues dance and play, teasing and yet voracious. I can't get close enough. I can't kiss her deep enough. It's like I'm starved and desperate, and only she can sate my hunger.

My other hand grasps her shoulder, but it barely manages

to hang on as it coasts inward until it's wrapped around a puffy jacket-covered breast. It's the most absurd thing, and yet the barrier only seems to rev me up higher until I find myself tearing down the zipper that's keeping me from them and sliding in.

"Fuck. I've always wondered what they'd feel like," I murmur absently, and it's as if I'm speaking to my teenage self. But she clearly likes it too, because suddenly she's hiking up on her seat and shooting over the console until she's practically on top of me. I laugh into her mouth. "He never did this with you, did he? Snog with you in a car like a teenager. Make it so you didn't know how to stop."

She shakes her head, not wanting the kiss or the connection to end, and neither do I, so I keep kissing her and kissing her until my lips feel bruised, but even then, I don't want to stop. Finally, I force myself to push her back into her seat so I can catch my breath and regain control of my fucking mind that I lost inside her mouth.

Suddenly I'm winded, my heart racing, and though I know most of it is related to the kiss, there's also this other part that's not.

"I had this whole vision in my head," slips out, but I let it die there without extrapolating on it. Because that vision... it's changed completely from what it was only moments ago. I imagined taking her home and fucking her brains out. I imagined putting her on the kitchen counter and eating her out, and then having her ride me in front of the fire while I watched the flames dance across her skin and her tits bounce in my face.

That vision was easy and simple. Dirty and fun.

But now... now I want to keep kissing her simply so I can taste her. So I can feel her breath and touch her hair and swallow her sweet little sounds that make me smile in fucking delirious happiness because I'm the one she's giving them to.

This new vision of her... it might be the death of every-thing—everyone—else. After that kiss, that vision is an entirely different beast than it was before. I can't remember the last time I felt anything close to that from a fucking kiss.

That kiss woke my soul and startled my senses.

"And now?" she questions, picking up where I left off, her lips red and swollen and her hair mussed from my hands. So fucking sexy, it's taking everything in me not to leap onto her seat and kiss her all over again.

*Now I need a moment to get my shit back together.*

I hold the shaky breath I just inhaled deep in my lungs before expelling it slowly, *willing* myself to calm the fuck down. "Now I only want to take it further because there is *nothing* even remotely boring or lame about your kisses. Those are the kisses men go to war and are willing to die for."

Her eyes round, shocked by my bold declaration, but I don't let it go anywhere as I lean over and kiss her again because I didn't mean to say that aloud. I never cared much about the kissing. It was always something else that never held the appeal of other more alluring things, but kissing her is poetry in my head. I want to sit down and strum on my guitar and write the perfect lyrics and notes that speak to how this feels.

Which is why I force myself away—for a second time—and then take note of a sign at the end of the street. "Oh, pictures with Santa. Let's go."

"What? Santa?" She blinks, her eyelashes fluttering at me like butterfly wings, but I need a minute or twenty after that kiss so I can rearrange my thoughts and bring them back to firmer ground. Back to the place where I remember that she's *not* mine, and this is all a sexual game. And I think the frozen air of this town might just be the ticket.

"Yes. Santa. I bet that ruddy old bloke will love having an elf like you sit on his lap."

She rolls her eyes. "Har, har. I'm not that small."

"I beg to differ, princess. But let's do this, and then maybe we'll find a pub for a drink, and I can order the design I have in my head for your naked body, and we'll see where this night ends up." The words blurt past my lips in a messy rush.

She takes me in as if I'm crazy, which I just might be. But I've never kissed a woman and lost my mind at the same time. So I need Santa now more than when I was a kid and used to wish for a bike or whatever I was after.

"O-okay."

I force a smile, ignoring the perplexed look on her face. "Grand. Let's go."

Before she can question my basic sanity, I fly out of the car and then come around to her side, opening the door and helping her down.

She peers up at me. "Are we good?"

"How do you mean?"

"You seem a bit... frazzled."

*Because I kissed you and realized your mouth might be what I've been missing my whole life.*

"I'm good." Then I laugh. "You know, I haven't checked the post we made earlier." Which feels strange that I haven't considering I've been glued to my socials for the last two weeks since all this blew up. Being with Faina, having brunch with her, conjuring up a playhouse of dirty deeds—it's taken my mind off everything.

I'm not sure what this week would have turned into out here all by myself, but I'm glad she's here. I'm glad it's not just me anymore.

"You should," she tells me, and I frown.

"Why?"

"Just take a look."

I drag us onto the sidewalk and keep my head down as I pull out my phone and bring up my Instagram app. "Bloody hell, over five hundred thousand likes and eight thousand comments?"

"It seems to be working," she comments dryly.

"Seems to be," I mutter absently, and then smile at her. "You're a genius." I land a hasty kiss on her lips without allowing myself to linger. "First Santa, then I'll buy you a hot chocolate. Possibly spiked."

"Deal."

We set off down the street, and I keep my head down and my body close to hers. Despite the Western vibe and the fact that it's bordering on one of America's greatest national parks, it's a very affluent town. Lots of women wearing designer threads and men decked out in posh winter attire. It's heaven.

Why you might ask? Because wealthy people find it beneath them to acknowledge or give credence to other wealthy people, especially celebrities. We are the lowest rung of wealth, which makes this little Western hideaway so much better than anywhere else. There is no press here. It's just wealthy people, families on Christmas holidays, locals, ski junkies, and us.

I hold my little minx's hand—it's cute and warm in mine, and I like how it feels—and lead us both toward Santa. I don't even know why I'm bothering at this point. We're out of the car, and I'm not focused on the epic kiss now that she's not practically on top of me with her tits in my hand. I have one memory of Mum and Dad pushing me onto his lap and screaming bloody murder the entire time.

Still, I think it will be adorable to see Faina sit on Santa's lap.

We get in line behind a dozen or so other children brave enough to manage the subarctic temperatures. I start pulling things up on my phone and discover there's a wealth of winter fun to do here. "I won't go skiing," I tell her. "But I'm willing to try snow tubing."

Her face lights up, and my chest clenches in the oddest way. "You will?"

"Definitely. It looks fun. There's also this Gand Teton winter tour thing we could try, though that might be bloody cold. But perhaps if we go a bit pissed first, that would make it more fun, so I'm in if you are."

"You're the eye before the storm, aren't you," she says to me, so deadly serious that it takes me aback for a moment. "I'm about to get blown over. I started this, and now I'm scared you're more than I can handle. I'm a twig scattered on the ground, and you're the wind and the rain and the fury."

I cup her jaw. "Princess, there isn't anything you can't handle. You're the ship no one can sink. Strong and fierce and fucking gorgeous. Don't let anyone ever tell you differently. Where did the woman who propositioned me for sex go?"

Her face heats, and she looks away. "She got the hiccups."

I grin. "Then tell her to hold her breath until they're gone." I inch in. "No wait. I'll scare them away." I take her by the hand, spin her out toward the center of the green space, and then haul her back in just before she stumbles on the edge of the sidewalk. She screeches, a gasp of a cry escapes her lungs, and then I drag her back into my chest. Without thinking, my hand finds her cheek, and I'm bending down and finding her cold lips with mine.

She's a bad idea, but those have always been things I've raced toward instead of running from.

"Are they gone?" I ask against her lips.

She smiles. "I was going to tell you Santa would have terrified them away."

I laugh even though we've grown a small audience. "Shhh. We're next. He'll hear you and not grant your Christmas wish."

I bob my head to the left, and sure enough, Santa is less than amused with us, and the line of people behind us even less so. I shove Faina toward Santa, and she drops onto his lap like a six-year-old. Except she's not. She's a gorgeous woman, and once Santa gets over his ire, he fully appreciates it.

His hands find her thighs, and then he's turning her, asking her what she wants for Christmas as if he's about to hand-deliver her presents just for her.

She tells him she wants to find joy in the small things and excitement in the things she never saw coming, and with that, she manages to steal a piece of me. Because I've never heard someone put it so simply yet so beautifully. Isn't that what life should be? Joy in the small things and excitement in the things we never saw coming?

A laugh hits the snowy air, even as I start snapping pictures of her. Because she is joy in a small package, and she is the excitement I never saw coming.

"I don't know about a small package," Santa tells her, his white cotton beard twisting to accommodate his dirtbag smirk and his bespectacled eyes gleam as they take her in. "But I'm happy to bring you all the joy you're searching for this season."

"Oi!" I snap, the bark climbing past my chest. "Back off there, mate. That's my elf. Not yours."

Santa looks as though he's about to challenge me on this. I get a cheery, smug grin as his grip on her waist—practically on her ass—tightens. "Isn't that up to the elf? She's the one sitting on my lap, not yours."

Faina looks shocked, but I don't even hear her sharp retort as I start for him when I hear clicks behind me and remind myself that as unfortunate as London jails were, I have to imagine US ones are even less accommodating. So instead of breaking his nose, I jump on his lap and then hold up my phone to take a selfie of all three of us.

Santa makes a pained noise under my weight and tries to shove me off, but Faina is loving it, and isn't that the point? I snap two pictures and then steal her away, running us over to one of the antler arches already lit up with white lights barely shining through the gray, snowy day.

"So much for a low profile." My lips slam down on hers, and the moment her hands grip my jacket and her tongue meets mine, all those jitters I felt in the car before are gone, replaced with good old-fashioned lust. "Can I take you home?"

"I thought you'd never ask."

## Chapter Six

Faina

DEX IS SINGING. He's driving us back to the rental—after promising me he'd be able to drive on the correct side of the road in the white stuff—and now he's singing. And tapping his fingers and generally appearing… I don't know. Not nervous per se, but something.

I slip out my phone and text Ava.

**Me: How's Will?**

She replies immediately.

**Ava: Not great, but not awful. I'm praying I don't get it because it doesn't look like a whole lot of fun.**

**Me: I'm praying along with you. Did you know Dex was going to be here? That Will promised him the rental house as well?**

**Ava: *emoji of devil grinning* Of course I knew. I was sitting next to Will when he told him about it.**

I stare at my phone, reading the message again, because surely my sister wouldn't do that to me.

**Me: AVA!!!! What in the hell?!**

**Ava: ::Evil laugh:: What? Brooks was a douche from day one, and you needed to step out of that and have a bit of fun. Who better to do that with than Dex? The man doesn't know the definition of laying low and could use you to balance him out a bit and keep him out of trouble.**

**Me: He nearly just attacked Santa!**

**Ava: But I'm positive you stopped it.**

**Me: He stopped himself.**

**Ava: See, already a positive influence. Besides, Dex has always had a thing for you, and you could definitely use being on Santa's naughty list this year. It's time.**

My face flushes, and I quickly glance over at Dex. He's singing and tapping and very focused on driving without killing us. I return to my phone.

**Me: He has not always had a thing for me.**

Stupidly, that protest doesn't stop the butterflies swirling in my stomach. If anything, they're in hyperdrive because I'm literally headed home to have sex with him. Who does that? Who makes plans to have sex with a rock star? One lousy text from my ex, a few self-deprecating thoughts, and now here I am.

Without regret, just loaded with nerves.

But the way he kisses… ugh. Those kisses were freaking magic and lightning in one. I'm almost afraid of how good he'll screw if that's how he kisses.

**Ava: Riiiight, you'd know better than I would because it's not as if I'm his best friend's wife or anything. *eye roll emoji* He's always had a thing for you but felt you were way out of his league and far too good for him. Now take advantage of that and get yourself laid by someone who knows what a clit is.**

**Me: How do you know he knows what a clit is?**

**Ava: Please. I've heard the stories about Dex Chapman same as you have. Even in high school, he was known for giving girls orgasms, and high school boys are helpless. Thank God Will is his best friend and coached him young. Plus, we both obviously watched that sex video.**

**Me: Fine. But what makes you think we're going to have sex?**

**Ava: This is how...**

A picture of Dex kissing me by the antler arch comes through, and I gasp. "No!"

"What is it?" he questions. "Everything okay with your sister and Will?"

"How did you know I was texting Ava?"

He gives me a sideways look. "Because I'm not a fool."

"Oh, no?" I flip my phone so he can see the screen, and he jerks the wheel, causing us to slide. "Shit!" he hisses, righting the car when we both go flying about.

"Asshole! You could have killed us!"

"Sorry! I wasn't expecting that. Warn a man next time."

"Warn you?! You kissed me on a public square after nearly attacking Santa. You knew people were snapping pictures."

"I didn't know they'd get that." Then he laughs and shrugs. "Oh well. Seems we're now dating."

"Dating?! I didn't agree to date you."

He rolls his eyes. "Not for real, princess. Just... you know... on social media or whatever."

"Um. No. That wasn't part of the deal. You said we'd been seen together and that it would spread rumors, but after the week, those would fizzle out when nothing came of it. Something came of this."

"And yet you allowed me to kiss you and said you wanted to go home with me. We've been kissing and touching all morning, and none of it has been covert. Face it, love. You're my woman now." His eyebrows bounce suggestively.

"Dex, this isn't a joke."

He groans, pulling off his gray beanie and running a hand through his sandy-blond hair. "Fai, it's not the horrible thing you're making it out to be either. They'll call us a rebound, and after the first of the year, they'll move on." He laughs then. Rather loud. "I don't even have a PR person to put out a statement, so the wheels on this will spin until I hire someone new."

"Fantastic," I grumble.

"*You* could be my someone new."

He's smiling, quite pleased with himself.

"No, thanks."

"Honestly, I'd love it if you'd consider the job. I'm not joking. I pay extremely well and need someone who knows what the fuck they're doing and isn't an evil, manipulative bitch."

I move closer to the window, folding my arms over my chest. "I live in Boston."

"London is better."

"No, it's not."

"You don't have to live in London to be my PR person. You'd just have to fly in anytime I needed you, which might be all the time." He winks at me. "You never know."

"No, thanks," I repeat, staring out the window.

"You already said there isn't much for you in Boston now. It's a real offer. Think about it."

He lets it die there, and a few minutes later we're pulling into the house, and he shuts off the car. Reaching over, he takes my hand and turns me to face him.

"Are you really angry?"

"The world thinks I'm having a holiday fling with a rock star."

He tilts his head, treating me to that devilish, crooked smile complete with irresistible dimples. "Well, you are."

"But I didn't want the world to know that! A few pictures

of us together in a friendly way is one thing. Us making out on the street is another."

His fingers run along my cheek. "What are you so afraid of, Faina? Why is the court of public opinion so important to you?"

"Because I want to be respected. Who's going to hire me now? Who's going to respect me now?"

"Princess, respect is earned and not given. You want them to respect you, be someone who demands it. Be a force of nature who owns herself and her life and doesn't allow others to dictate how you do things. Ever. One thing I've learned in this business is that haters are going to hate. People will always have an opinion, and oftentimes, it's not favorable. But that's on them. It's their problem to deal with, not yours."

"So says the man who orchestrated this so we'd be seen together, and it would improve his public image."

"That's for my endorsements. For my label. This is my career, and unfortunately, my career is tied to my public image. But as for me? I don't regret breaking that arsehole's nose, and I don't regret sacking my bitch of an ex. Frankly, both did me a favor because I knew I wanted out with her for a while but couldn't find a way to do it. It just happened to backfire on me. But you, my adorable little elf, you have nothing to be ashamed of. You're a woman, fierce and strong and proud. Own your sexuality. Own your life. And make no apologies for it."

He's right, of course. I've been living my life for others. So afraid of the court of public opinion that I've been too scared to do much of anything for myself. Who else am I living this life for other than myself? When I'm old and gray, I don't want my life to be overshadowed by my regrets. I thought the same thing this morning, but it's time I don't just think the words, it's time I believe them.

It's with that thought that I attack him.

I launch myself across the console and drop most of my

body weight onto Dex's chest. He gives me a fantastic grunt and then quickly catches up as his mouth claims mine and his hands meet the sides of my head.

"Do you want a safe word?"

I pull back on a wet gasp. "A what?"

He's laughing at me. "A safe word."

"Are you into BDSM?"

"I mean, if you're asking if I want to tie you up and spank your arse red while making you come, the answer is yes."

"If that's what you plan to do, I can tell you with one hundred percent certainty I do not need a safe word."

"Oh, love, we're going to have the best week together."

Just not more than that. The thought makes me inadvertently frown, and I hate that. Like *hate* it! A boyfriend or commitment is not what I'm here for. So I need to get over it. I'm just used to that style, is all. That's why my insides suddenly feel like they're twisted into knots at the idea of this ending after a week and him returning to England without me.

Pushing all that aside, he drags my mouth back to his, his tongue immediately seeking entrance into my mouth and thrashing against mine.

"Do you normally have a safe word with your lovers?"

He smiles against my lips. "No. Never. I just wanted to see your reaction. I swear, I'm not into the lifestyle or anything. I just like a bit of fun and kink with my sex." Then he kisses me some more, his hands in my hair and on my shoulders, and impatiently ripping at my coat as his mouth consumes mine. My hands aren't to be held back either. I'm tearing at his zipper and raking through his hair, and feeling so frustrated by the confines we find ourselves in I can hardly stand it.

"Inside?" I groan into his mouth.

"Yes," he pants, sucking my bottom lip into his mouth and nibbling gently on it. "Now."

Both of us race out of the car, slamming doors, and then

as I round the car, Dex scoops me up and tosses me over his shoulder, making me yelp in surprise.

"You're going to drop me!"

He laughs. "You're half my size, princess. I won't drop you. You move too slowly with those short legs."

"I do not!"

"Not fast enough." He races us up the front steps, punches in the code for the front door, and then once he has us inside, he lets me slip down his body. Suddenly it's quiet. So quiet. The only sound is our heavy breathing. He stares down at me, green eyes burning with heat, a fire so bright I can't help but match it, burning equally as hot for him.

I've never wanted anyone this way.

I don't know if it's because he's an unexplored crush from once upon a time or if it's because he's a famous rock star or because he wants me or because it's just him. Dex. No one has ever looked at me the way he's looking at me.

No one has ever wanted me like this.

It's not an act. It's not desire for the sake of desire or being horny. It's desire for the other person. It's a wanting so fierce and penetrating there's only one way to extinguish it. In an instance, we launch at each other, clashing with teeth and lips. His hands finish the job of unzipping my coat, and mine do the same with his.

We break apart to undo boots, and a laugh slips past my lungs. "This is ridiculous."

One boot goes flying and then the other, and then we attack again, unable to handle the distance for a second, only for him to break the kiss to kick his other boot off that was hanging from his foot. He pulls hard on my hand, and I stumble into him, and just when I think he's about to devour me again, he slows down, his fingers grazing along my jaw.

"You're so beautiful," he whispers reverently, and then his mouth dives in, his lips and teeth worshipping my neck, making me arch into him. His hands slip down, grasping the end of my sweater and pulling it up and over my head. "Fuck," he hisses, pulling back so he can take in my bra-covered breasts. "I saw this on the bed earlier"—his finger runs along the lacy edge and swell of my breast over it, his eyes trailing the motion—"and I saw your tits too, but I swear, I was not prepared for how gorgeous these are."

He lifts both of them, squeezing and pressing them together. His face plunges into the pillows of cleavage he created, licking at the crease.

"Christ, the way you smell." He takes a deep inhale of my skin. "I need to taste you. Turn around and give me your perfect arse."

## Chapter Seven

Dex

IN A FLASH, I tear myself away from her magnificent tits and then spin her around, forcing her hands flat against the wood planks of the door. Her breath catches high in her throat, and I can't help my satisfied grin. I reach around and undo her button and fly, and then slowly, so fucking slowly, slide her trousers down her hips, over her plump arse, until they're latched around her ankles.

Reflexively she steps out of them, shoving them out of the way with her foot. She's breathing so hard, from being worked up, or from nerves, I'm not sure which. Her forearms press into the dark wood door, her forehead leaning between them as she stares down at the floor, averting her gaze from me. The voracious princess from the car is back to being my shy rose, but that won't keep for long.

I take a step back and groan at the sight before me. Long blonde hair, wild and messy down her back. Pale skin, white lace, and curved hips. And her arse. Sweet mother in heaven, it's so bloody perfect I can hardly stand it.

Just like the rest of her.

I take a step forward, my hands rubbing the globes of her arse, and I lower myself to my knees. Far from the most comfortable position given the inhospitable floors, but the way she squirms in front of me is well worth the discomfort.

"Has anyone ever done this, love? Eaten you out from behind?"

A head shake. That's all she's giving me.

"Good."

My fingers twine in the thin strings on either side of her hips, and then in one fast motion, I tear her underwear from her. Before she can even formulate a noise or a response, I'm spreading her cheeks, tilting her hips back toward me, and burying my face inside her pussy. She shivers against me as she cries out. My fingers knead the soft globes of her arse as my tongue plunges up inside her tight cunt, and I immediately groan.

Because *fuck*.

How is this real?

How did I get lucky enough to be stuck in the same cabin with my high school crush, and she just so happens to ask me to be the man to help her into a sexual awakening? I feel as though I should go out and play the lottery or hit up Las Vegas.

She has no clue about all the ways I want her. I would have given anything for a shot with her back then, and now this is the chance I never thought I'd get or was entitled to.

I won't pretend to imagine anything beyond this. I've been burned, and so has she. It's a week of fun and a week of pleasure, and I plan to deliver both to her. But I can already feel that I'll miss her when this is done. And I know the taste of her, the smell of her, the *feel* of her will be etched into my mind, never to be washed away or replaced.

It's that thought that tightens my grip and has me diving in deeper, licking my way around her clit. She's moaning and swiveling her hips and reaching behind her back to rip at my hair. She can't decide what to do with me back here, eating her this way, and it's absolutely fantastic.

"I can't get enough of the way you taste." Like skin and soap and so fucking feminine and perfect, my cock pulses with a singular need. *Her.* "I'm going to suck on your pussy until you beg me to stop."

I trace my finger to her clit, playing with the swollen, sensitive nub as my tongue thrusts in and out of her. Her legs shake, and the noises she's making I already know are the first of their kind to come from her.

A man has never taken his time with her. He's never eaten her cunt just to taste it and feel it and watch as she comes undone. He's never wanted her the way I want her, and it makes me angry. And pleased.

Angry because she's my age and has likely never had good sex until now. Pleased because I'm the one to finally give it to her. Speaking of…

"Please," she whimpers, crying out against the door as I pick up my pace.

Her sounds are my total undoing, and I dive deeper into her like a man possessed. My hand holds her ass open, my nose practically pressed against her forbidden hole. I let my finger slide inside her, switching things around and sucking her clit into my mouth. Her thighs spread wider to accommodate me, opening herself up, and I smile against her wet flesh before I blow cool air on her.

"Ah. Oh, my hell."

"That's it." I pump in and out of her, rubbing my finger against her front wall as I do. "You're so tight, Faina. I need to put my cock in you and feel the way your pussy grips it."

"Dex," she pants, her head falling back.

"Yes, love. Tell me what you want."

"I want…" she trails off.

"You want me to make you come?"

"God, yes."

"You're so sexy," I purr against her, licking at her clit. "You like it when I do that, don't you?" She whimpers, and I suck her clit into my mouth, feeling her pussy quiver against my finger as I fuck her with it. "I love how wet you are for me. Push your arse back toward me. I want to feel all of you. Your body is mine tonight."

She shamelessly grinds against my face as I increase the pressure on her clit while adding a second finger, curling it, and rubbing her inner spot. All I can breathe—*all I can taste*—is her. An intoxicating drug along with her moans and pleas and cries of pleasure. I suck on her clit, using my tongue to play with it. Her thighs shake, her knees ready to give out, and her hand claws at the door.

Flicking her clit with my tongue one last time, she comes, muffling her scream in her arm as she writhes against my face. My hips thrust forward into empty air, aimlessly seeking only what she can provide. Then something washes over me. A memory. She sags against the door, her chest heaving as she attempts to catch her breath.

Victory surges in my chest as a self-satisfied smile curls up my lips. I feel giddy. Euphoric even. I made Faina come, and like the teenage boy she makes me feel like, I mentally high-five myself for it. She's so beautiful, so bloody perfect—all fucking mine.

I give her pussy one last kiss and then slide my fingers from her, sucking them into my mouth. "I fucked my bed and came all over my sheets when I was seventeen, picturing doing exactly this to you."

Her head flashes back, and she rips at my hair, forcing my head back. Her eyes are owl-wide, dark blue, and saddled with lust. "You did?"

I laugh at her bewildered expression. "Princess, you were the prettiest girl in our school. The smartest too. I never stood a chance with my rubbish grades and bad boy tendencies, but that didn't mean I didn't notice you, and that certainly didn't mean I didn't want you. Whether you believe it or not, I thought about you a lot when I was alone in my bed."

The flush on her cheeks intensifies, and suddenly she's spinning around to face me. I stand, towering over her, yet she manages to knock me down to nothing when she places her small hand on my chest over my pounding heart and stares up into my eyes.

"You mean that?"

"Absolutely."

She grins. "Catch."

"Pardo—oomph." My lungs empty as she jumps up into my arms and wraps her legs around my waist.

"I'm not that heavy."

"You're a feather in the wind, little elf. Does this give me the freedom to carry you upstairs? As much as I'd love the wildness of fucking you down here against the front door, I think I might enjoy splaying you out on a bed so we're able to reap the full benefits of positioning."

I don't give her the chance to answer. Instead, I spin us around, gripping her by the upper thighs just beneath her arse, and then head for the stairs. My mouth attacks hers, wanting her to taste herself on me, but also, I don't know how to not kiss her for longer than a minute.

Her kisses are drugging. They're euphoric, and with every pass of her lips and tongue, my skin buzzes and my insides hum. It's the same sensation I get right before I take the stage. Like my body knows something truly amazing is about to happen, and I don't want to miss a second of it.

I jog up the steps, taking them at a pace that jostles her body and makes her yelp when I bite at her breast that's right in my face. This bra has to go. I don't know why I left it on all this time. I could have already had her naked. I could have had unfettered access to these beauties, and I've wasted precious seconds here.

"You need to strip," she demands as we reach the summit of the stairs and I walk her into the bedroom.

"Funny, I was just thinking about how I need to remove your bra so I can have you fully naked."

I set her down on the bed and stare with such uncontrollable lust as she reaches behind her back and unsnaps her bra. The straps slip from her petite shoulders, one and then the other, and the cups follow suit, revealing her stunning breasts before she tosses it who cares where.

"You're never to wear a bra again," I say, the words shooting out.

Her head tilts, her long hair cascading over her chest, covering one nipple. It's the ultimate tease. She looks like one of those Renaissance paintings. "I sort of have to."

I shake my head. "Not while we're here then. In this house, I will need constant access to these." And then I shove her back onto the bed, climb on top of her, and capture one pretty pink nipple in my mouth. This woman tastes like fucking candy. Like the goddamn sugar cookies she made this morning.

One hand comes up, lifting the heavy swell of her other breast in my hand, testing its weight, already knowing I'm going to fuck these magnificent things. I groan at the thought and switch to her other breast while using the pad of my thumb to rub the wetness I left behind all around her nipple. She's flat out, thighs spread, knees hiked up on either side of my hips, hands in my hair, eyes closed.

"You're still dressed," she gasps as I bite down on her nipple. "Please, Dex. I want to see you. I want to touch too."

I puff out a breath, my forehead falling to her chest, and then I force myself back, taking in the lovely creature beneath me, and I feel it in my chest. A pinching. A tightening. A foreboding spasm. Something that's telling me this could get out of hand, and I should run now.

Only I know that's impossible.

The last six hours with her have been the most fun I've had in far too long and I don't want this to end. It's just the madness of the past few weeks that's ramping this up in my head. That's all that is. I'll take her a hundred times over this week, and it'll be enough because it has to be, and then we'll both walk away with fond memories and nothing more.

Or maybe we'll be those people who meet up every so often and have a fling.

But that's all this can be, and I'd do right by both of us in remembering that.

I reach behind my head and pull my T-shirt and jumper over my head. I toss them aside, and then she's sitting up, her hands immediately going to my abs, palms flat as they slide their way up to my pecks and shoulders.

"You have a lot of ink," she says admiringly.

I gulp at the feel of her hands on my bare skin and nod. Her touch is like fire, sizzling a path over me and leaving burning embers in her wake.

"Is it a rock star thing or a Dex thing?" she questions, and my eyebrows bounce in surprise. No one's ever asked me that. They've always just assumed it's because I'm a musician.

"A me thing," I tell her, taking the long strands of her flaxen hair and pushing them back over her shoulders. "Each one symbolizes something to me. An era I went through. Like a chapter in my life, I don't want to forget, whether good or bad."

She swirls a finger along the angel wings I have on my flank, and I shudder, making her smile. "What's this one? It's different from the others."

"I got it when my mum died five months ago."

Sadness lines her features, and I trace the twist between her brows down to the dip of her upper lip. "I didn't know. I'm sorry." She lifts her chin to kiss the tip of my finger.

I smile and lean down to take her lips. "I called her after Will's wedding. Told her what I said about you that day. She

64

called me a miserable git who didn't deserve your air. She wasn't wrong."

Faina snickers. "I always liked your mom, though I only met her a few times."

She kisses me back and goes for the button and zipper of my trousers, and suddenly we're back to that frenzy we can't seem to escape for long. Our lips kiss messily as she shoves my trousers and boxer briefs down over my arse and hips until my cock springs free. My fingers toy with her wet pussy, rubbing her clit in earnest as I use the balls of my feet to kick off my trousers. I kneel on the bed, climbing in between her thighs and pressing my hands into the mattress on either side of her head as I kiss her. I grind into her, feeling her fucking incredible wet heat on my swollen cock, only to growl in frustration and pull away.

"What is it?" she breathes, watching me with dark eyes as I go for my wallet.

"Condom," I grit out, my cock angry and leaking.

"Hurry!"

I smirk but feel the same urgency as I flip through my wallet and produce the foil packet.

I turn back to her, staring at the goddess before me. "Spread your legs, Faina, and show me how badly you want me."

"W-what?" Her cheeks flush the loveliest shade of rose as lust and uncertainty battle across her face.

"Show me exactly what you want me to do to you. I want to see how you want my cock to fuck you."

"Oh, God," she hisses, her eyes closing and her head tilting back.

"Come on. Do it. Fuck yourself. Show me how deep you want me to go."

She shudders and then hesitantly glides her hand over her body, sliding it down until she's cupping her mound.

"Wider, Faina. Spread your fucking legs and show me

exactly how you want to get fucked. I swear it, I'm going to make you scream in pleasure, but I want to see how naughty my good girl can be first."

"Fuck." She makes a strangled noise, and then she spreads her thighs wide and slips two fingers straight into her cunt. My cock jerks, practically smacking my abs as if to say, "Hey, remember me, that's where I'm supposed to go." My breaths come out choppy and ragged at the erotic sight before me.

Never have I seen anything sexier in my life than Faina fucking herself to my command.

With my eyes on her pink pussy and glistening fingers, I tear open the condom with my teeth and sheath myself up, absently shaking my head at the way my hands tremble as I do it. In a flash I'm back on her, standing at the foot of the bed as she continues to pump her fingers in and out.

I bend down and swirl my tongue around her clit, and she whimpers.

"Please, Dex. I want you inside of me. So badly."

Christ. This woman. "I can't wait another second to slide inside of you, princess. Eyes on me as I do."

I raise her calves until they're nestled on my shoulders, and with my hand wrapped around the base of my cock, I line myself up and then slowly push into her all the way to the hilt.

My lungs empty, and sweat immediately coats my brow. "Christ, princess, you have the tightest fucking cunt." My jaw locks so I don't shoot myself into her now. "Are you okay?" I ask because her back arches and her hands shoot up over her head, grasping onto the bed linens.

"Ah! You're big."

"Best compliment ever, but are you okay?"

With her eyes pinched tightly shut, she nods.

"You sure? Because I have to move or I'm going to die. It's a certifiable fact." As it is, my voice already sounds like I've run a marathon and lost.

"Move," she commands, her eyes slashing open, and

pinning to mine. "I want to be fucked. Please. I need this too. Remember your assignment. I'm here to learn all the best ways to fuck, and that means you can't go easy on me. I want you to tell me exactly what to do to get you off."

"Jesus," I hiss between clenched teeth. "You're a goddamn dream, Faina. There is nothing even remotely boring about you. Fucking nothing." Sliding back, I stare down at where her wet pussy grips my cock like it's its long-lost lover, and then I push all the way back in, thrusting up as I do.

She moans, her eyes closing and her head going flat against the white duvet.

"Yes. That. Is that good for you too?"

Is she kidding? "It's fucking heaven."

And then I start to pound.

Hoisting her up, I move her until her arse is off the bed and her knees are on my shoulders, and she can't do anything other than take every inch of my cock as I slam it into her. Her tits bounce and sway as her body repeatedly swallows my cock like the good little girl she is. Only I don't want Faina to be good. I want my little elf to be very, very naughty.

I want her to not just take but to give, and to give the way *she* wants to.

"Princess," I hiss through my teeth because *fuuuuck*, I'm in her deep, and *fuuuuck*, she feels good. "I want you to ride me."

She blinks open her glazed eyes. "Ride you?" The words are a foreign language on her tongue as she repeats them.

"Yes. I want you to fuck me. I want you to show me what you like."

She shakes her head, and I start to slow down, grinding in and out of her, swiveling my hips. "I don't... isn't this so I can learn how to not be boring?"

Jesus. What did that twat do to her,? I wrap her legs around my waist and then lean forward until our chests are pressed together and my face hovers inches over hers. I roll into her with short, upward thrusts that make her eyes roll back in her head, but I cup her jaw and force her eyes straight back to mine.

"You are not a robot. You are not a vessel for my pleasure or any man's pleasure. There is nothing sexier or hotter than watching a woman getting off and knowing you're the one doing that to her. If a man takes from you without giving and then has the fucking audacity to call you boring, *he's* the shitty lay. Not you. I swear to you now, there is nothing boring about watching you ride me. It'll be the show of my life. There is nothing for you to learn that you don't already know. It's experience, confidence, and the right partner you're lacking, nothing else."

My hand slips beneath her back, and then I'm rolling us on the big bed until she's sitting astride me, my cock still deep inside her. Her eyes flare when she feels how deep she can go like this.

With my hands on her hips, I lift her and drive her down on me just as my hips thrust up.

"Holy! Ah!"

"You like that?" I rasp, barely hanging on.

She nods her head over and over and over, her hands slamming down on my chest, fingers spread. "Can you do that again?"

"Sweet princess, I've got all night and all fucking week to do that again."

She starts to bounce as I start to fuck up into her, and I wasn't kidding when I said watching her like this would be the show of my life. Her hair, her flushed skin, her tits, the way her pussy is spread open, giving me the most depraved, lewd view of her... I groan, wanting to taste her again.

Over and over, I fuck her like this. Hard. Rough. So deep I'm buried to the hilt. Our bodies pumping, seeking, destroying as one. Her pussy drinks my cock in, sucking it deep and holding on for dear life. She's tight. And hot. And fucking wet. And Christ, her pussy is the silkiest slice of heaven I've ever experienced, and I tell her that as I continue to drive into her.

"Fuck. Fuck. Fuck." It's a rhythmic pattern I can't stop as she bounces on me. She rolls forward so her clit can slide against my pelvic bone, but I like her upright, so I pop my thumb into my mouth, getting it nice and wet, and slide it between us, rolling her firm clit.

"Ah! Dex!" she cries, and *yesss!* Hell yes! I'm fucking Faina, and she's loving it and I'm loving it, and I never ever want this to stop. She feels too good. And where she was fucking the wrong men, I was fucking the wrong woman and the wrong women before her.

Faina's pussy feels like it was made for me.

Her body starts to spasm, her pussy clenching my cock to the point where I see bloody stars behind my eyes, and then she's coming spectacularly. All over me. Writhing and whimpering and moaning and losing her balance and falling forward for me to catch her. All the while I continue to pound up into her until I'm coming equally as hard, bellowing out her name like she's the answer to all my prayers.

Her body sags, both of us panting for our lives in thick, heavy gasps. I lick the sweaty crevice of her shoulder, moving the mane of her hair away so I can get better access, but it's not enough, and I turn her head so I can reclaim her lips.

"You still with me, love?" I ask, smiling at her dopy smile.

"Somewhere, possibly over the rainbow, way, *way* up high."

I chuckle, and she giggles, which makes her pussy clench, in turn making me groan. My cock is already pleading for round two, though I know it will need at least five minutes before we can rise to the challenge. With one last kiss, I slip out of her and go about disposing of the condom. Something I'm going to need to purchase in bulk.

By the time I return, ready to snuggle and then fuck my

little Christmas elf into another round of orgasms, I find her up on her feet, sliding into leggings and a red jumper.

"What in the name of Santa do you think you're doing?"

She blinks at me, a radiant, beautiful smile lighting up her face and making her blue eyes glow. "Getting dressed." She gives me a devilish once-over but then moves on to brushing out her hair. "You should too. It's a gorgeous snowy day. Let's go have some fun in it."

"Some fun in the snow," I echo because surely she must be kidding. Or still high in some post-orgasmic bliss.

She skips—*bloody skips!*—over to me and lands right in front of me, planting her chin in the middle of my sternum and gazing up at me in a way that has my chest clenching and my breath tight. "Let's go on an adventure. I have the perfect place in mind."

Oh, hell. I'm in a lot of trouble with this one.

## Chapter Eight

Faina

I FEEL like I woke up in some crazy Hallmark holiday film—
obviously, a smutty one—but one where fantasy takes flight
and reality is suspended and the girl spends the week with the
world-famous, insanely gorgeous, and incredibly good-in-bed
rock star. The rock star who never fails to make her smile or
fill her with butterflies or remind her how she deserves better
than she's gotten.

But, with that incredible movie, I have to remind myself
that even though I'm technically that girl, it isn't real. And
unlike with Hallmark, Dex and I won't have a happily ever
after. Despite what the tabloids are now saying. My phone
started lighting up like Rudolph's nose with texts from friends
back home as well as Ava.

So even though he doesn't know it, I'm taking measures to
safeguard my heart. That means no lingering in bed. It means
sex without intimacy after. Because while I may be suspending
reality for a while, I refuse to get hurt twice in the same week.

At some point, I'll have to figure out my next steps, but

that will have to wait until after the holidays. For now, the bonus of all this is that Brooks hasn't called me again, so that's likely done and over with.

"Where are we headed, princess?" he questions, putting me in the passenger side and then running around to the driver's side and getting in. He starts the car with the press of a button and then turns to me.

"I was thinking a gondola ride," I tell him. I saw a brochure for them on the counter of the shop he dragged me into, and I looked it up quickly on my phone when he was using the bathroom, and it sounded incredible.

"A gondola ride?"

"It climbs up the mountain and gives you views of Yellowstone Park and the Tetons."

He blinks at me. "You mean the metal box contraption that is suspended hundreds of feet in the air and is only held there by a metal cable as it climbs up into the mountains that are covered in snow?"

"Yep. Sounds great, right?"

He's staring at me as if I've grown three heads before his eyes. "Great isn't quite the word I would have gone with."

"There's a restaurant at the top." I bounce my eyebrows. "I believe it serves alcohol."

He flashes me a wicked grin. "Are you trying to get me pissed?"

"If that means drunk, then possibly. But come on, it'll be fun. And beautiful. And quite frankly, you owe me."

He squints at me. "I owe you? How do you mean?"

"The world thinks I'm your favorite flavor, and judging by the pictures, I'm no longer vanilla." I slide out my phone, pull up the tabloid link Ava texted him, and show him the picture of us making out by the antler arch. This is a different picture than earlier. "Evidently, we put on quite the show for the townspeople."

He grins at the picture, not the least bit put off by it. "Did you read the caption?"

"Unfortunately, yes."

"They're already declaring us in love."

My lips form a flat line. "I'm aware."

"And a couple."

"I see that."

"Not just a holiday fling," He starts reading the article, "Sources close to the couple claim their relationship is already serious. Childhood sweethearts Dex Chapman and Faina Spencer appear more than a little cozy together during their holiday escape after reuniting only weeks after Chapman's very public breakup. Could this be a second chance at love for Britain's premier rocker?"

He rubs a finger along his lips that dip down at the corners. "Only Britain's premier rocker? Why not the world? I sell far more in the US than I do in the UK. Hell, I sell out bloody stadiums."

I make a noise in the back of my throat. "I think you're focusing on the wrong side of this. They only mentioned a recent breakup. No arrest. No scandal. No cheating. The PR rep in me is loving this for you and thinks you should make another IG post that perpetuates this notion. But as the woman you're appearing more than a little cozy with, I'm nervous this will all blow up in our faces."

"And you think being trapped in a cage suspended high over a mountain range is the way to fix that?"

I shrug. "Certainly, can't hurt."

"I beg to differ on that." His eyebrows scrunch, and he tilts his head. "Wait, who are these sources, and how does the press already know we knew each other as kids?"

"My money's on Ava."

He belts out a laugh. "You think your sister turned state's evidence on you?"

I toss my hands up in the air. "Who else?"

He catches a lock of my hair and starts running the strands through his fingers. "True. Will has the flu, which means Ava is bored and spending too much time on her phone. And it would never occur to Will to speak to anyone about my love life, nor would he care enough to. My agent and manager know nothing of you, and I don't currently have a PR manager, as we know."

"As we know."

He gives my hair a tug and treats me to his crooked smile. "A gondola ride and a drink then, eh?"

"At least one."

"Gondola ride or drink?"

"Yes."

In a flash, he's yanking me toward him, and his mouth crashes into mine. A groan splits his lips, and then his tongue is trying to do the same with mine, begging for access. This kiss is different than all the ones before it. This kiss is an apology for the pictures and articles. It's a plea for me to stay and stick this out with him regardless. It's a kiss that says we might be in a bit of a mess, but we're in it together.

"Forget why you're starting to think this is a bad idea," he says, clearly reading me. "Forget the tabloids and the nonsense of the outside world. Get lost with me here, princess. I promise I'll take care of you. I won't let any of this reflect poorly on you. Ever. I just don't want you to run."

Despite my desire for distance, I melt into him and kiss him back, wordlessly capitulating to his every demand. I am lost with him here. And I have no plans to run.

It's too late for any of that anyway, and frankly, I still don't have any place to go.

He holds my face in place, kissing me soundly, and then in my next heartbeat, he's backing us out of the driveway and steering us toward the ski resorts. We park in the lot, and then with both of us all bundled up, he takes my gloved hand and leads us toward the line of people waiting to get on.

"Oh, hell fucking no."

I laugh. "Don't tell me *the* Dex Chapman is afraid of heights."

He stares apprehensively at the gondolas as they shoot into the air, swaying ever so slightly as they do.

"Heights? No. Enclosed spaces dangling like a worm on a hook? Absolutely."

"I'll protect you."

He shudders, his head shaking ever so slightly. "How long is this ride you're dragging me on?"

"Twelve minutes or so."

"Too short to have sex," he declares, and the woman in front of us turns around with a blazing scowl. "What?" he says to her plainly. "It is."

She glares at him until recognition lights her face. "Are you Dex Chapman?"

He gives her his most charming smile. "That depends on your angle. Fan or press?"

She blinks rapidly. "Fan. Huge fan!" She spins and grabs her friend's arm, yanking on it and forcing her to turn.

"What?" her friend snaps, shaking off the grip on her arm. "We're next."

"Bethy, look. It's Dex Chapman."

The other woman's eyes round. And then she screams. Like at the top of her lungs, sounds as though she's being murdered on the streets scream. "DEX! OH MY GOD! I LOVE YOU SO MUCH!" She launches herself at Dex, who manages to catch her without toppling over into the snow. She squeezes the life from him, and then her friend rips her away for her own shot.

"Can we have your autograph? And a selfie? And your firstborn?" She laughs in a way that suggests she's kidding, when I think we all know she's anything but.

Dex chuckles good-naturedly. "Yes, to everything. Except the firstborn, of course. I'm hoping my lovely childhood sweetheart over here will do that for me. You know, since we're in love."

That son of a bitch. I stomp on his foot, and he throws me a Cheshire grin.

"Oh, hi." Both women finally realize I'm standing here in the cold beside him. "Yes," the first woman continues. "We saw the pictures. How cool is this? We're never anyplace these things happen. Are you really together? I mean, we know what happened with your ex." She cups her hand over her mouth, staring all around as she says the last part.

Dex laughs it off. "None of what you saw with my ex was as it happened. She was a cheating, miserable snake of a human. But who cares about her? I've reunited with the love of my life. What's more Christmas than that?"

"You slimy motherfuc—" He cuts me off with a searing kiss, and my knee immediately comes up, landing straight in his balls. He oomphs and then grunts into my lips, squeezing my arm as his face twists in pain. "You deserved that," I say against his lips.

"I did. Thank you for not going full force, but that love bump still hurt. It's the situation we're in, princess. Might as well have a bit of fun with it."

I shake my head, and he smiles, stealing another kiss, and then suddenly our gondola arrives, and the line shifts ahead, even as everyone has their phones out, taking pictures and videos and likely posting them across the planet. Awesome.

If he isn't the most playful, gorgeous, infuriating ass on the planet...

"Dex! You get to ride with us!" Bethy is still shouting, but Dex's eyes are all over me.

Dex drops his hand to her shoulder and leans in conspiratorially. "Actually, love, would you mind terribly if we took up the box of death—I mean, gondola alone? I want to try and prove my twelve-minute theory wrong." He gives the women a wink and that dimpled smirk, and they swoon accordingly. "You know how new love can be, especially over Christmas."

"Sure! Of course. Wow. You really are insanely gorgeous."

"Aw, thank you, darling. So are you. And to show my appreciation..." He slides a marker out of his pocket along with a notebook and starts scribbling things down as the guy running the gondola urges us on. Pieces of paper tear, and then he's handing one to everyone around us, all the people who were about to board the gondola with us. "Here. These are for you. That's my manager's business phone. Give him a ring, and tell him I told you to send each of you a promotion box. Make sure you give him the code I put on there, or he'll never believe you."

Eyes light up like New Year's in Times Square, and no one argues about the two of us cutting the line and taking a box meant for at least twenty by ourselves. Frankly, I don't either. Once again, I find myself needing a moment. It's only been a day, and yet everywhere we go and everything we do ends with us making a scene in one fashion or another.

Everyone takes their turns with selfies, and Dex never rushes anyone. He's all smiles and easy laughs, and I realize he loves this. He loves connecting with fans. And he's good at it. That's why the world turned against him so quickly. He has a bad boy, sex god reputation, sure, but he's never been a bad man. He's good to his fans and does charitable work and is generally considered a good human.

So the notion of him cheating and unnecessarily hurting a man sat all kinds of wrong with his fans. Vindication is price-less and when he turns his magnetic eyes on me, I can see the gratitude and joy in them. A warmth I'm unfamiliar with spreads through me, lightening my chest and curling a smile up my lips.

Dex tugs me onto the gondola, and then the door swooshes closed, and we're encased in delicious heat that makes me shiver and sigh at the same time. Then I turn on him, only his hands are already out protectively.

"Remember, if you get me with a second shot to the bollocks, it'll only hurt you tonight."

"I can't believe you did that." My arms flail, even if I'm having a hell of a time fighting my amused grin.

"Will you break my nose if I tell you this might, in fact, be the most fun I've ever had?" He takes a cautious step in my direction just as the gondola shoots forward, propelling us up into the air. He grabs onto the glass wall, his eyes wild with fear. "Christ, princess. Look at all that."

I stare out the window, taking in the sweeping snow-covered mountains and breathtaking landscape. "I should break your nose."

He moves carefully in behind me, pressing his chest to my back and wrapping his arms around my body, his chin on my shoulder as he holds me, and we lean against the window.

"What good is living if you can't have some fun with it? We only die once, and in case you've missed it, I subscribe to the carpe diem model."

"Clearly I never took Latin."

"But you're learning all sorts of new languages today."

I sigh and then laugh lightly. "I don't want to be old when I'm this young, and I'm all for fun, but it's getting out of hand."

"It is," he agrees. "I know it is. I sort of feel as though I got early parole from prison, and the taste of freedom is perhaps a bit too intoxicating. I tend to get swept up in the moment and carried away with myself. Right now, quite literally. Fuck, we're high. Jesus, what the bloody fuck did I let you drag me into?" His grip on me tightens.

"I thought you said you weren't afraid of heights."

He pants out a short, choppy breath. "I lied, didn't I? You wanted to go on a bloody gondola into the mountains, and I wanted to make you happy because you're insanely stunning when you smile at me. Not to mention, if I'm being honest, I don't think I could ever say no to you, so here we are," he rambles as if he can't stop the words from pouring out. "Me, two seconds from having a massive panic attack. You, angry and gorgeous and ready to chop off my cock and feed it to the local bears."

I cough out a laugh, and I don't know if it's the fact that he got on this gondola with me even though he's afraid of it just to make me happy or the fact that seeing the world from this vantage point naturally brings about an inner peace, but I relax against him.

"I'm not going to chop off your cock. Or break your nose. I'm just not as comfortable being the center of attention the way you are. Of the two of us, Ava was the sun, and I was content being the moon, and that hasn't changed."

"Ah, but the moon you can stare at. The moon won't burn your eyes with her beauty."

"Dex—"

"I'll cool it," he promises. "At least I'll try." He sucks in another breath. "Fucking hell, how high are we? I can barely breathe in this thing."

I remove my gloves and do the same with his, stuffing both into my coat pocket, and running my fingers on his hands, which are now clenching my waist as if he's holding onto me for dear life. He might be panicking, and I do feel bad about that, but I'm entranced by the snow falling and the earth at the base of the mountain growing smaller.

"Try closing your eyes."

"Right. Sure. Like that will somehow trick my mind into forgetting *I'm in a moving box thousands of feet above the ground and am likely about to plummet to my death.*"

"Didn't you mention something about sex and trying to prove yourself wrong with the twelve-minute window?"

He puffs out a laugh, his face diving into my neck as his lips start to kiss and suck on my skin even though he's still breathing hard, practically hyperventilating. "I do perform well under pressure, but we've already wasted precious minutes. Perhaps I'll just make you come to atone for yet another public scene I dragged you into. Are you still mad?"

"No," I admit.

I stopped being mad when he gave me that look right before we stepped on, and I forgave him the second he started to panic at the height. No one's ever done anything just to make me happy or smile.

"It's never dull with you, is it, Dex?"

I can feel his smile against me. "Nope. Never. You should see me on stage." His hand slides in front of me, unzipping my jacket. My hands move to the glass, splaying out in antici-pation. My heart picks up a few extra beats as nerves and excitement war within me.

"I have," I tell him, my breath hitching as his hand starts to sink into my leggings and beneath my thong. My hands press firmer against the glass, suddenly needing support when my knees feel like they're about to give out on me.

"Oh?" he remarks, surprise in his husky voice. "When was that?"

"Two summers ago, when you came to Boston." I gasp as he circles my clit, and then plunges two fingers straight into me.

"Mmmm. So fucking tight and wet." He plies my neck with kisses. "I wish I had known you were there. Did you like the show?"

"No." The word comes out as a moan. "I hated it because I hated you."

He chuckles, biting my earlobe. "Yet you purchased a ticket to my concert."

His fingers continue to pump in and out of me, slowly, as if we're not climbing higher, and time is on our side. "I went with a friend and never told her I knew you."

"Well,"—he licks a trail up my neck—"she certainly

knows you do now." He quirks his fingers inside me, pressing firmly against my front wall while his thumb presses in on my clit at the same time, making me cry out. "It's only us in here, princess. You can scream as loud as you want. I want you naked so badly. I want you naked and wet and begging for me to fuck you. But for now, I want you so loud that every animal and human within a thousand miles knows what my name sounds like as you scream it."

Only I can see we're getting closer to the summit. I can see the peak in the distance, close enough that soon people will be able to see us. "Dex... oh god!" I whimper when he starts working my clit and thrusting in and out of me faster with every go. My body is shaking as heat curls through me, my fingers pawing at the glass. "We're nearly there. People will see soon."

"Is that what you want? People watching as I make you come?"

Fuck. Is it? The thought makes me moan, and my toes curl in my boots. It sends a rush of wet heat straight to my core. He feels it and groans, rubbing his hard cock against my lower back. I want it inside me. I want to feel him fuck me again so badly I can hardly stand here.

"Oh, princess. I think part of you would like that very much, and we can play with that a little later. But for now, if you don't want them to see you come, then you better do it quickly because we're not getting off this gondola until your cum is coating my fingers." His other hand comes up, wrapping around my neck and holding me against him without cutting off my breath. "This isn't going to be enough for me. Touching and kissing and smelling you. I need more. I can't get enough; I have to have more."

"Me too," I pant, as his fingers play with my pussy the way he plays his guitar, skillfully and coaxing. He's groaning, thrusting into me with his hard cock as he ups his pace, rubbing furiously against my swollen clit. The noise is wet and sloppy, and I want more. So much more. I want to rip his clothes from his body and take his cock in my mouth. I want to lick every line and crevice and ridge of his abs and chest.

But in return, I want his mouth and hands all over me. The way they were just a couple of hours ago. He's stoked a fire in me I never knew was burning and now I'm a new woman.

I reach behind my back and grip his cock, squeezing it until he hisses out a harsh breath, right against my ear. The sound is so hungry and primal, that it sends me over the edge in a rush.

"I'm going to come," I warn him seconds before I do. Shaking and writhing and trembling. I'm loud as he wanted me to be, but now the threat of being heard is very real, and he uses my jaw to turn my face and kisses me fiercely, suffocating my moans and whimpers.

"That's it. You're coating my fingers, and it's so fucking hot. I'm throbbing for you. You feel that? It's your dripping pussy doing that. Your cunt is mine, Faina. Fucking all mine."

I ride his hand, grinding into it, needing more as my orgasm goes on and on. His filthy possessive words, along with where we are and what we're doing, have my body in hyperdrive.

"More, Dex!"

"Naughty fucking girl." He fucks himself into my hand, and I moan into his mouth. "I'm going to drag you into the bathroom of the restaurant and then force you onto your knees. My sweet little princess is going to swallow every inch of my cock. Aren't you, love."

"Yes!" I gasp for air as my eyes roll the back of my head. No one has ever spoken to me this way, and it's exactly what I want. I want to make someone depraved and greedy. I want them to be so hot for me that they don't know how to hold back.

After an eternity, I'm utterly spent, practically collapsing against the glass just as the gondola slows at the top of the summit.

"Holy shit," I gasp, my head turning and my eyes opening, taking in the mountain top through the glass. The car comes to a stop with a smooth jolt that stirs me back to where we are. Dex's fingers slide out of me, and he releases my neck, turning me around, and then he slides one finger in my mouth, making me suck myself clean off it, and then he takes both fingers that were inside me, and I watch as he sucks them.

Fuck, that's so dirty and so hot. I lick my lips, tasting my cum just as the doors of the car slide open, and a burst of frozen air hits us. But before we can exit, his mouth comes down on mine, kissing me ravenously, both of us tasting me on each other.

He pulls back, but I'm still dazed, my legs like jelly beneath me. I lick my lips, and he purrs at that, dragging me into his side and then leading us off the gondola.

"Land at last, though I imagine this contraption is the only way down?"

"Unless you want to ski."

"Not a snowball's chance in hell, little elf."

Our boots crunch in the firm snow, and the wind whips wildly around us, making us both huddle closer together. He turns me and zips up my coat for me, then takes our gloves from my pocket and puts mine back on me first and then his. I blink and try very hard not to overthink how caring and tender that gesture is when he didn't even do it to be so.

He did it because he wanted to make sure I wasn't cold.

"This was your grand idea?" he asks, tucking me back into his side and walking us toward the restaurant. "Freeze us to death? My cock was long and thick and aching for your mouth, and now the poor bloke is crying, begging for warmer climates."

I giggle lightly. "Is my mouth not considered a warmer climate?"

He gives me a side-eye with a raised eyebrow. "You get very playful after you come."

"So I'm learning about myself. It's all new for me."

He stops short and twists me until I'm standing before him, my back now to the restaurant I'm anxious to get inside.

"What does that mean? So you're learning?"

I tilt my head, squinting against the bright, cloudy sky. "I don't understand your question," I admit.

"You've had orgasms before. Right?"

"Of course."

He blows out a plume of vapor in the form of a relieved breath. "Fantastic. You had me worried for a moment there."

I shrug and we start back off. "But only with myself before you."

## Chapter Nine

Dex

I COME TO A SCREECHING HALT, making a couple behind us nearly bash into me in the process. I don't care about their displeased grumbling. Or even the cold any longer—though it's certainly no joke and likely to cause frostbite very soon.

"What do you mean you've only ever had an orgasm with yourself before? Explain. Now."

She stares at me as if I'm a wild creature, but I don't care.

"What's there to explain? You're the first guy to ever give me an orgasm from sex, and the guys I've been with before did a little foreplay, but not a lot, and they never seemed to care what I liked or didn't." She shrugs haplessly. "It didn't feel the way it does when you do it, and it never... you know... led to that."

"Faina..." I trail off. "Can I see your mobile for a moment?"

Her eyes narrow. "Why?"

"Because that slimy, sniveling, wormbag of an ex of yours called you boring in bed when *he's* the one who never gave you an orgasm. Faina, that's just…" I shake my head in furious disbelief. "It's criminal. But what's worse is that he made you believe that you were the problem and not him. I've been with you for *one day*, and I can tell you with one-hundred percent certainty that you're the best sex I've ever had, and not to sound crass or even bragging, because it sort of comes with my job, but I've had a lot of sex with a lot of different women. I wanted to hurt him before for making you doubt yourself—because no man should ever have that sort of power over you—but now I intend to kill him with my bare hands, and I need your mobile so I can call him and find out where he is."

Faina blinks her pretty blue eyes at me as something passes across her features I can't quite read. In a flash, she's grabbing my gloved hand and marching me toward the restaurant. She plows us through the doors and tells the host we need a table for two in the back.

The kid doesn't so much as blink in my direction, which is a relief, as he grabs two laminated menus and walks us through the restaurant. I keep my head down and angled away—a natural instinct at this point—until we reach a round table with a high-back semi-circle booth.

"Perfect," she exclaims, and then all but shoves me in, pushing me along until I scoot in to make room for her.

The host hands her the menus and leaves, and I turn on her. "Are you going to explain?"

"Shhh," she hisses at me just as our waiter arrives, pouring water into our glasses and greeting us. "Not yet," she whispers to me under her breath.

"Would you like a drink while you look over the menu?" he asks.

"Can we have five minutes? My boyfriend and I are just finishing up an argument."

"Oh, sure," he says, his eyebrows shooting up in surprise and a little discomfort. "I'll be back."

He walks off, and then Faina turns on me. "You have to promise to do something for me."

"Uh, all right. What is it?"

"The idea of kneeling on a bathroom floor grosses me out, but I want to do this so badly I can't wait. Coach me through it so I know what you like and remember to keep as quiet as you can."

Words and confusion catch in my throat for approximately two seconds. Because that's all it takes for her hand to start rubbing my still semi-hard cock over the zipper of my trousers. My balls instantly draw up, already aching and needing release from what we did on the gondola.

"Princess," I rasp, trying—I swear I'm fucking trying—to maintain some semblance of rational thinking, but it proves nearly impossible with all the blood in my brain shooting down to fill up my cock. She peers up at me through dark lashes and gives me a coy smile that will haunt me for eons to come. There is no way I can deny what she's about to do.

I want it too badly.

Even in a restaurant with hundreds of people around us.

"Take me out and lick me."

With eager, obedient fingers, she undoes the button and zipper and then slides her small hand into the soft cotton of my boxer briefs. She grips the base of my dick, frees him, and then bends under the table to run her tongue from the base all the way up to my tip, where she swirls her tongue around the fat head of my cock.

I hiss, one hand flying out to grip the table, the other finding the thick, glossy mess of her hair. I can't remember the last time Elsie went down on me. Ages at least, but I swear to all that is holy, once again, it never felt like this. So hot and wet and timid, which somehow only seems to make it more wickedly sinful.

She does it again, flattening her tongue on the sensitive underside, her head ducked beneath the table, and I can't believe Faina is sucking me off in a crowded restaurant. It's unfathomable and easily the hottest thing that's ever happened to me, and I've pretty much done everything.

"That's it, love. You can suck me now. Take me down your throat as deep as you can until you gag. I want to hear it. I want to see that moment in your eyes when my cock is too much for your pretty little mouth."

She moans, her eyes swirling with heat, and I groan, even as I try to fight it. Her mouth... hell. Her mouth is going at me like sucking cock is her favorite sport, and she's in it to win it. Her head dips down, diving as far as she can go, and when I hit the resistance at the back of her throat, she dutifully gags and then swallows, and I swear, Santa and his reindeer fly behind my eyes and promise me the world in her mouth.

She pulls off with a wet pop, catches her breath, throws me a look that could make me come right now, and then dives back down as deep as she can go once more. I can't stop the groan this time. The way she's sucking me down and bobbing on me as if there has never been anything better in her mouth has me smacking the table and shooting my hips up.

I cannot believe Faina—my good girl Faina of all people, the most beautiful woman I've ever seen—is doing this, and that only makes it hotter. My hand runs through her hair, brushing the strands back from her face and clasping them in a makeshift ponytail. I want to see her face and the angle is already crap for that given the confines of the table. Quickly my gaze scans out, making sure no one can see what we're doing, but the table they put us in is perfect.

We're completely shaded by the high booth and its curve, so I return my focus to my princess, already starting to wonder after only one day how I'll let her go at the end of the week.

She dips back down, and I hold her there for a second, my eyes burning with heat as tears start to line hers. A shudder wracks through me as I slide back out, her cheeks hollowing and lips dragging as I do.

"Motherfuck, Faina. Jesus, that's good. You are perfect. So bloody perfect, I can hardly stand it."

Her hand wraps around the base of my cock, and she starts stroking me deeper into her mouth. With her doing this, with us being here, it won't take me long. As much as I want this to last and last, we simply don't have the leisure of it.

"You'll do this again later," I tell her through clenched teeth as sweat breaks out on my forehead. "Only I'll be eating your pussy while you do. Shit."

I bring my fingers that were inside of her up to my nose, inhaling her scent, and that's what does it. The smell of her, the mental image of Faina sitting backward on my face, the magnificent way she's sucking and gagging and swallowing and licking me has my hips bucking, my grip in her hair tightening, my balls drawing up, and my cum shooting down her throat.

She chokes and gags but continues to suck and swallow and finish me off until I'm nothing but hers. Soft and compliant and utterly spent. Using my grip on her hair, I pull her up, cup her jaw in my hand, stare into her breath-robbing eyes, and kiss her. Deep and hard and more passionately than I think I've ever kissed a woman before.

I chuckle against her lips. "How has it only been one day with you?"

It feels like ages. Like months and years, and yet at the same time, not nearly enough. This week won't be nearly enough as there is no limit to the things I want to do with her.

"All made up now?" the waiter asks, and I laugh against Faina's lips as I shift forward so he can't see my softening cock that's still out.

"Yup. All good," I declare and glance over to him. "Sorry, mate. We need another few minutes. I promise, we'll make it worth your while."

Recognition lights his face, and there will be no privacy for us this week unless we make our own.

"Oh, sure, man. That's great. Take all the time you need. I'll be over there." He points to a far corner. "Just signal whenever you're ready."

"Thanks. We appreciate that." He scuttles away, his face already on his phone, and I groan. And then laugh as I go about tucking myself back in and zipping up. I turn back to her. "Where was I?" I move in to kiss her again, but she pulls back.

"People will start to watch us now that he's recognized you."

"Right." I tilt my head, still unable to remove my smile. "So, I shouldn't kiss you then?"

She pushes in one of the dimples on my cheek. "Nope. I'm going to the restroom. Then let's order because I'm starving."

"My cum was just an appetizer then?"

She rolls her eyes, but I follow after her, needing the loo myself. I do my thing and wash my hands, and by the time I return to the table, she's not yet returned. I start to glance over the menu when I get a text from Will.

**Will: Fevers suck, and I feel like death, but this is my PSA to you that if you hurt my wife's twin, otherwise known as my sister-in-law, I will be forced from my deathbed to kick your British rock star ass back across the pond.**

**Me: Sorry you're feeling dicky, mate. Best wishes with that. And fuck you in your arsehole, because I am not going to hurt Faina. We're having fun, and neither of us is looking for anything more. You should know, I'd never hurt her.**

I bristle, ready to start typing more to him but stop myself. He's just looking out for Faina, and I appreciate that, but I am too. She asked me to help, and that's what I'm doing, and in doing so, she's also helping me. It's mutually beneficial, and we're both in the same place on this. With an expiration date.

That's growing closer and closer with every passing second.

**Will: You mean because you've secretly been obsessed with her since you were fifteen and learned all the fun you could have with your dick while thinking about her?**

I roll my eyes like a child.

**Me: I've not been obsessed with her.**

**Will: What would you have called it then? You used to watch her like a creeper.**

**Me: Did not.**

**Will: Did too. And Ava agrees with me. It's why she never told Faina you had a crush on her, even though everyone knew you did, with the exception of Faina.**

**Me: What's that supposed to mean?**

**Will: I think you know.**

I grunt, tossing my phone on the table face down. A strange, uncomfortable sensation washes over me, but I quickly shove it aside, glancing up just in time to watch Faina exit the loo and head back toward me. Her face is down, her eyes shadowed, giving me the opportunity to watch her unobserved, and that sensation comes back, only this time it slams straight into me.

Was I obsessed with her? Have I been all these years?

I wanted her at Will's wedding. I couldn't hide it, and Elsie saw it. But I remember feeling thunderstruck when she walked into the church. I hadn't seen her since school, and there she was, and I remember wanting to rush over to say hi. I didn't, of course. Instead, I was a miserable prick to her and spent the night trying not to think about the way her hand felt on my arm as I escorted her down the aisle or the way her small body fit so perfectly against mine when I was forced to dance with her.

I resented Elsie that night.

I resented her because I protected her feelings instead of Faina's. I resented her because she was there, and that meant I couldn't talk to or look at Faina. For months and months after, I resented her for that. But I also knew my resentment was futile. There was a reason why Ava never mentioned to Faina that I had a crush on her, and I was all too aware of it.

I was a bad boy, and she was a good girl. We all knew she deserved better, and I didn't dispute that. Plus, she was out of my league, and I didn't dare to imagine she'd ever return my affections. Over the years, Will would mention Faina in passing, and I'd jump all over him like a dog seeking a treat for any tidbits I could gather about her.

I knew she was in Boston.

I knew she was in PR and marketing.

But it was just something that was there. Useless thoughts that lingered in the back of my mind with no chance of becoming reality. Except now, here we are.

She pops down onto the bench and scoots in, picking up her menu and perusing it. I'm holding mine, though I can't tell you anything on it. My heart is too busy pounding in my chest. And that strange sensation… it's everywhere.

"Do you have a Christmas wish?" I ask her out of absolutely nowhere.

A bemused sort of giggle tickles past her lips. "A Christmas wish?"

"Yeah," I continue, nervously licking my lips and gripping the menu just a bit tighter. "Something you wish would come true that you only ask for this time of year since it's the only time of year where it doesn't feel silly to do so. Something that feels impossible, but you'd give anything to have."

She leans back against the booth. "I don't know," she says softly. "I'm not sure I've ever thought about it like that."

But I can see it in her eyes. There is something.

"Go on," I push. "You can trust me with it."

She sighs and then glances down at her hands still holding

the menu. "I guess I'd want to run my own company. I've thought about it off and on over the years, but the timing never felt right. Not to mention the risk that comes with it."

"And now?"

Her eyes come back up to meet mine. "And now I'm not sure. The timing feels better, but the risk is still there, and I don't know how to do that in Boston after what just happened. I'm likely making a bigger deal out of it than I should be, but maybe this was all fate's way of telling me it's time for a change. That I should take the leap and not be afraid."

"Do you believe everything happens for a reason?"

"No," she answers quickly. "My parents are dead, and I can't think of one reason for that to have happened." Her parents died in a car wreck when she was at university.

I nod in concession because I feel exactly the same way about my mum and dad. "I don't either, truth be told. But I do believe that sometimes fate steps in when you need it the most."

"What's your Christmas wish?" she asks, and my immediate thought is *you*. Because I think it might be. I think Will is right, and I've wanted Faina for as long as I can remember. And she's here, right in front of me, both of us escaping our lives at the exact same time.

"To be worthy of all the special and beautiful things of this world and to grab on with both hands when the right opportunity is in front of me."

I may not believe everything happens for a reason, but I do believe fate brought us together. I just have to find a way to prove it to her.

## Chapter Ten

Faina

DEAR SANTA, all I want for Christmas is for my hot holiday fling with the bad boy rock star to not break my heart. Is that too much to ask for? After we ate waffles and drank beers, I managed to get Dex back into the gondola and down the mountain, and then we walked around town for hours, holding hands and laughing and talking about not a whole lot.

It was the easy sort of conversation you have with someone when the words don't stop flowing and you just seem to be on the same wavelength with practically everything. We went back to the house and had more incredible sex and then fell asleep, and I woke up sometime around four in the morning—hello, jet lag and time change—to find Dex wrapped around me like a vine.

After that, I couldn't fall back to sleep, and by the time he woke, we had more sex and then had breakfast and went snow tubing down the mountain. We took lots of adorable selfies, and Dex posted them, but it doesn't even matter. The world knows where we are, and any time we're spotted out, that picture inevitably ends up online somewhere.

Thankfully, the press can't get here. There is not a room at any hotel to be had, and as Dex previously tried and failed, there are no rentals either. Thank God it's Christmas. Which is actually tomorrow, making tonight Christmas Eve.

I've been thinking that I should get Dex something, but I have no clue what. What do you get a rich rock star who can buy himself anything he wants?

"You truly want to do this?" Dex questions as we stroll through town. Light snow is falling all around us, and the air is a balmy thirty degrees compared to yesterday's twenty.

"I do," I tell him, beaming a big smile I can't stop. "I haven't had an excuse to cook a holiday meal in years, and it's something I used to do with my mom when we were younger. Ava hated cooking, so she and my dad would go ice skating at the mall or something while my mom and I made a Christmas Eve feast."

"I'm rubbish at cooking," he admits. "I have a cook because otherwise, I'd eat nothing but carryout."

"So you're saying you won't be helping me in the kitchen."

"I'm saying you'll be thankful that I don't. But how's this? I'll buy all the ingredients, and a few bottles of wine and champagne, and perhaps a nice bourbon."

I snicker. "That's a lot of alcohol."

"It's Christmas, princess. That requires a lot of drinking, and we're here through New Year's, remember."

"How can I forget," I quip, though my voice comes out more strained than I intend it to. These few days with him have been the best of my life, and I know we have another week together, but I'm worried either a week won't be enough, or it'll be just long enough for me to get seriously hurt.

I haven't even thought of Brooks since his last text the other morning, and I was with him for five months. Dex is consuming, and all-encompassing. He's rewriting things inside me I haven't given him permission to. It's effortless and ridiculous with how fast it's happening. Like I slipped into a time warp and suddenly I'm back in high school, and the only boy to occupy my thoughts is him.

"I'm not excited about that being the end of it either," he says, his voice soft and his face turned away from me.

That takes me by surprise, though I don't know why. Dex seems to say his thoughts as they hit his brain without much of a filter. It's sort of how he leads his life too.

"You're not?"

He turns back to me with a wary half-grin. "No. I mean, I'd rather not stay in the frozen Tundra past this week, but I'm not all that anxious to return to London."

I want to ask him why not. I want to know if it's because of his ex and the situation he left there, or if it's because of me. I want to ask him that. But I don't.

"I feel the same way about Boston," is all I can manage because it's the truth. I've been thinking a lot about this over the last couple of days, and while I love Boston, I'm thinking it's time for a change. Possibly back to LA, or maybe New York, or... nope. Not going to even think about it.

"We don't have to, you know."

"Have to what?" I question as we enter the supermarket, and I grab a cart.

"Go back to Boston or London. We could go somewhere else. Together."

My heart skips a beat, but I ignore it. "I have to figure out work for myself, Dex. I have some savings to tide me over for a while, but that's it. I can't just take off like that, and I certainly can't travel around and blow through money."

"You know I have loads of money, right?"

I roll my eyes at him as I start for the produce. "It's always so hot when men brag about their money."

"No, I mean, I can pay for us."

I shake my head. "I can't let you do that. It's a sweet offer and part of me would love to say yes, but I can't keep putting off figuring out my next steps."

He frowns, but thankfully lets it go there. I find the romaine lettuce and then cherry tomatoes, all the while Dex watches me shop as if it's a novelty he's never witnessed before.

"What precisely are you making for us?"

"Grilled Caesar salad, herb-crusted beef tenderloin with horseradish sauce, truffle mashed potatoes, and Brussels sprouts. And something chocolate for dessert."

He groans. "Careful, love. You're tempting my heart through my stomach, and I'm a willing victim."

Funny, he's tempting my heart through my head, and I'm trying not to become a victim.

"Also, I might have scheduled a few things for us tomorrow."

That catches my attention. "Oh?" My eyebrows meet my hairline.

"Right, so I had to pull a few strings, but I've secured us a spa day with massages and other fun treatments, and then a traditional Christmas dinner. Though by traditional, I mean American and not English, which hurts my soul, but there you have it."

"Oh?" I repeat, this time putting a lot more inflection in my voice.

"Yes, and you're not to argue with me. I might have also purchased you a dress for the occasion." He leans down and smacks a kiss right on my lips. "I'm off to find the liquor. I'll be back before you pick out dessert." Another kiss, and then he saunters off, drawing the double-take of everyone he passes.

I slip out my phone and dial up Ava as I continue shopping.

"Well, well, if it isn't my internet sensation sister who turned my holiday rental into a love shack."

"I hate you."

She laughs. "For someone having regular sex with the seriously hot Dex Chapman, you don't sound happy."

"Ava…" I trail off, not even sure what to say.

"Why are you setting limits?" she asks because she's my twin and she knows exactly how my brain works.

"We both did," I protest. "That's the deal we made." Until he had to go and offer to extend it.

"And plans change. Just look at me. I'm sitting in my PJs watching black-and-white Christmas movies while my poor guy is upstairs feeling like shit and trying not to give me his plague. He won't let me in our bedroom. He's legit made me leave his meals outside the door. I love him for it, but it's Christmas Eve, and I *miss* him."

"How are you not sick of him after all these years?"

"Because when you find your person, any time you spend without them is wasted time. I'm never sick of him." She pauses. "Is that weird?"

"It's pretty great actually. We should all have that kind of weird in our lives." I walk along, leaning on the handle of the cart, picking up random items, and dropping them in.

"Faina, I'm not telling you to marry the guy, but you don't have to be so dramatic and pragmatic when you can simply be fucktastic."

I belt out a laugh, not even caring if anyone is looking. "Thank you. I needed that. And I'm trying. I am. I'm just…"

"Not built that way?"

"Exactly. You have Will, and you've always had Will, but it's a minefield out here for the rest of us."

"Wah. Boohoo, you have a gorgeous *rock star* hot for your poonani. Remind me to shed a tear while I cry for the dude in this movie who has legit problems."

"You're watching *It's a Wonderful Life* again, aren't you?"

"Shut up. You think you know me."

"And I bet you're also sitting in your Rudolph PJs, sipping

a margarita, and picking at nachos and tacos you had delivered because you don't cook."

"I hate you."

I cackle. "I miss you."

"I miss you too. I wish you were here. So you could make me food."

"I'm in the grocery store now. I'm making Dex what Mom and I used to make every Christmas." I start to get choked up and have to clear my throat.

"I'm super jealous. These nachos are soggy."

"I'm sorry. There's nothing worse than soggy nachos."

"Straight facts. I'm in California. That should be outlawed." She clears her throat. "Fai, he's not a bad guy. He's actually a great guy. Loyal and loving like a puppy dog. But like all puppies, he's a bit wild and definitely a lot, and I know that's not your typical flavor of jam, but give him a chance. He's legit had a thing for you since we were kids."

"Ava, you're assuming he wants something beyond a fling."

"I'm not assuming, Fai. I know he does. I also know you like him."

I sigh. "What's not to like? He's tender and attentive and gorgeous and fantastic in bed and funny and witty and so sure of himself."

"He can sing too. Did you know that?"

I roll my eyes. "Yeah, I knew that. He sings in the car while he drives, and he sings in the shower too." It's so adorable, I smile just thinking about it. And the way he kisses me or smiles at me with those dimples. And how he holds my hand everywhere we go or tucks me against him to keep me warm.

I have it bad for him, but that doesn't mean it'll translate into anything good.

I was looking for fun and excitement and to live, even for a little bit, without regret. I feel like I've been doing that. I'm happy. Hell, I'm having the time of my life. But there is no future with this.

"Already knowing his habits. How precious.

"Ava, please stop. It's not helping me."

"Ugh. Fine. Just… think about it. Don't discount the idea of being with him for real simply because he's an impulse dress you bought on a whim but so far aren't daring enough to wear."

"Huh?" M brows scrunch as I pick up a bag of Brussels sprouts.

"We all have that dress. That dress that's a bit too tight, or reveals a bit too much skin, or is so not us we know we'll never wear it, but we just had to have it. That's Dex for you. Try it on, Fai. You might just realize it's a perfect fit and so very you after all. I'm going to reheat my nachos, and refresh my margarita, and try not to cry that I'm not eating dinner with you. Next year. Love you."

"Love you," I force out and then slide my phone back into my purse. Because fuck, I miss my sister. And fuck, her words are slithering into places I'd rather them not gain access to. Only I force myself not to think about my sister's romantic notions for me with her husband's best friend. That's all this is. Wishful thinking.

I continue shopping, and true to his word, right as I'm in the dessert aisle, he appears. "This one," he demands, pointing to a tiramisu.

"You think?"

"Definitely. And just so you're aware, I might have gone a bit overboard in the shop."

I feign incredulous. "What? No. You?"

"I didn't know what sort of wine you like, so I took a flyer with a lot of different sorts. And champagne. And I know Ava likes tequila, so I purchased some of that too because I wasn't sure how far your twins thing ran."

"It runs far and deep. I love tequila."

"Can I lick it off your tits, and before you answer, it might be a fantasy of mine that's never been realized."

"Then obviously yes."

His crooked smile lights up his face, making his dimples sink in and my heart swoon. "You're my dream, you know." He nails me with a kiss that leaves me winded, and then we walk about the store together, shopping as if it's what we always do. He refuses to allow me to pay for anything, and then we're driving home, and I'm stuck in my head, even as he sings along to whatever is on the radio.

The moment we get home, he helps me unload all the groceries, puts on Christmas music for me, but I don't miss him retreating to the back of the house, sitting in front of the outdoor fireplace, and strumming on his guitar while I start making Christmas Eve dinner for us. I get lost in the task of prepping, cooking, and singing along.

It isn't until I feel him behind me, his hands on my hips as I take the meat out of the oven, that I realize how much time has passed.

"You get stuff done?" I ask, setting the heavy baking dish on top of the stove.

"I did, actually."

I twist over my shoulder and give him a big, beaming smile. "That's great."

"I wrote nearly two songs. I haven't done that in such a short time in ages."

"Will you play them for me?"

"Maybe later. They're still too new in my head, if that makes any sense."

"It does," I tell him, returning to the meat. "I hope you're hungry. I have enough food here to feed an army. We used to eat this on Christmas Eve and then have the leftovers for a few days. We didn't have the money for multiple big meals, so leftovers were our thing."

"It smells incredible." His lips slither along my neck, and

then he takes a deep inhale. "So do you for that matter. On a scale of zero to ten, how mad would you be if I got on my knees, bent you over the counter, and ate you instead?"

"Five."

I can feel his smile. "So, not angry enough to stop me from doing it, but just angry enough to punish me for it?"

"Something like that."

"Faina, put your hands on the counter."

"Or what?" I challenge.

"Or I'll make you."

## Chapter Eleven

Faina

I START to make a break for it, but his arm bands around my waist before I can get far, and then he's swooping me up and off my feet, twirling me through the air, and then slamming my ass down on the counter.

Immediately he's on me, his body between my legs, and then he's pushing me back, forcing me flat, his palm dragging down the center of my chest, between my breasts, until he reaches the top of my leggings. His green eyes are dark and fierce, predatory as they rake me in, noting my heavy breathing.

In an instant, he's ripping my leggings off, forcing a shocked cry from my lungs. One by one, he places each foot up on the counter and then spreads my knees apart, bearing me to him. He stares down at my thong, the thin scrap of pink satin that I'm positive is revealing a wet mark, like it's the most fascinating thing he's ever seen.

"Take off your shirt."

With trembling hands, I reach down and pull it up and

over my head. The stone is cold against my back, and I arch away from it, but his hand is there, pressing me back down and making me shiver once more. His finger grazes across the trussed-up swell of each breast over my bra as he tracks every line and curve I'm composed of.

"This is how I want you to eat dinner tonight. Only wearing this. But I want my cum leaking out of you as you do."

Holy Christ. My eyes close, and my breath hitches. "Dex—"

"You're on the pill. I saw them in the bathroom."

I nod my head, my teeth sinking desperately into my bottom lip, so I don't combust right here.

"I was tested after I caught Elsie."

"Brooks and I always used condoms." I open my eyes, noting his curious expression. "I've never had sex without one," I admit. Ever the cautious, good girl, I had a friend in college who got pregnant before she wanted to, and I didn't want that to be me if I could avoid it.

"Faina, can I fuck you bare?"

I shouldn't say yes. I know what it will do to me if I let Dex be the first person that I've ever done this with. But I can't help but want it to be him either. I give him a jerky nod, and then he drags me up by the back of my neck and slams his lips down on mine. His tongue dives into my mouth, taking no prisoners as he immediately overpowers me.

My hands grasp his shoulders, my body off-balance with my feet up on the counter this way. He continues to kiss me, holding me by the back of the neck, his fingers up in my hair as his other hand comes down, sliding over my breasts until one finger swirls over my clit through my underwear.

I whimper into his mouth as he pushes the damp spot into me, gliding up and down, toying with me. He's diabolically good at this. Every touch, every pass of his lips, every breath he gives me makes me more and more desperate for him. I ache, my pussy clenching, needing to feel him fill me up.

Needing to just feel... more.

He breaks the kiss, nipping at my bottom lip nearly to the point of pain. "Stay upright. I want you to watch me." With that he trails down my body, placing wet, open-mouthed kisses as he does, all the while his fingers continue to tickle and play with my pussy.

One hand lands on the counter behind me, the other in his hair as he reaches the apex of my thighs, and then takes a deep inhale of me. Adrenaline slams through me, making my skin prickle and my blood thrum. He pulls my panties aside, baring me fully to him.

"Oh, princess. How I love your pretty cunt." He takes another inhale, his nose rubbing my clit. He spreads my thighs wider, as wide as they can go, and then he uses the flat of his tongue to lick from my opening up to my clit. I whimper, gripping his hair tighter.

I never imagined I could ever feel beautiful and sexy being this open and exposed to a man, but Dex doesn't just make me feel beautiful or sexy or even desired. He makes me feel alive. Like I'm finally discovering the woman I've hidden beneath layers of fear and ingrained self-consciousness.

Since I walked out on Brooks, I've been shedding those layers one by one, but listening to Dex groan and grunt and watching as he eats me like a man starving, hungry and voracious, I think I finally shed the last one.

His fingers dig into my thighs in a way that makes me think he'll leave marks. I moan at the thought. At the notion of finding his fingerprints on my skin. A secret taboo only we'll know about.

I ache so fiercely for him I can hardly stand it, and I tell him that. The words tearing from my lips as his teeth graze my sensitive clit. He's rough. Rougher with me than he's been these last few days. He's testing me, I realize. Seeing how far he can go, but little does he know, I have no intention of stopping him.

This might be all new for me, but I already know I want it all.

He presses his thumb to my clit, his other thumb now holding my folds open and giving his tongue better access. I'm barely hanging on. Barely able to breathe. Fighting the urge to close my eyes. To stop watching. But I can't. The way his eyes flicker up to mine and then back down to where he's eating me is so overpowering it's as if my mind is caught, held in his possession.

His tongue swirls and swirls around my opening while his thumb rubs and rubs at my clit. I can't stop it. My orgasm slams through me, making me scream and rip at his hair. My thighs clamp against the sides of his head, the intensity too much, and yet I'm helplessly grinding against his mouth and thumb.

My grip slackens in his hair, and then he's standing, tearing his jeans down, and parting my thighs once more. He lines his cock up, moving the head around, using my arousal as a lubricant.

"Eyes, Faina. Give me your eyes. I want you looking at me when you feel my cock inside you like this for the first time." My head snaps up reflexively, and then without warning, he slams into me.

I cry out, my back arching and my arms holding up begin to shake. I can't breathe. I can't think. All I can do is *feel*.

"*Fuuuuck*, that feels bloody fantastic." He breathes out a harsh breath and then another as he holds himself still. "You feel that, love? You feel how deep that is? How fucking good? Christ, Faina, it's this. Nothing has ever been this good. Not ever."

I can only nod. It does feel different, and it's never been this good, and with that, he's ruined me. Not just because of the way it feels, but because of the way *he* feels.

His forehead falls to mine, our noses brushing as he starts to pump up into me. His eyes close, and his breath stutters. He pulls me upright, drawing me closer—any space between us is too much—and I hug him to me.

All the fire and madness from when he was going down on me is gone, replaced with slow thrusts and eye contact, punctuated by heavy breaths that mingle between our layered lips. I've never been close like this with someone while they're inside of me. Never made such fierce, unflappable eye contact. His lips eat at mine, and I taste myself on him. The pleasure is undeniable, and I start to whimper, needing more of it.

He pulls back and shoves in, harder this time, shifting my hips so our angle is deeper. So I'm more open to him. It's a tight fit—it always is—but somehow it's tighter, wetter, more intense.

"I'm so hard right now," he marvels, licking the seam of my lips. "You make me so hard, princess. I've never been so fucking hard in my life."

I can feel every inch of him. The way he throbs against my tight walls. The way he shifts his hips so he can reach that perfect spot inside me with every push and pump. He's still dressed, which makes this feel dirty and degrading, yet the way he's surrounding me makes me feel worshipped and adored.

Words slip past his lips, words I can barely make out. Murmurs and sound—almost like music—feed into me, stirring me up until I don't know where he ends and I begin. He makes me feel like I'm the only one in his universe, and it's such a fucking high that I'm gasping and whimpering and biting at his lips and begging, *pleading*, for him to make me come.

"Soon," he rasps, his face falling to my shoulder, his teeth sawing along my collarbone. "Soon. I want to feel your perfect cunt come on me, but not yet. It's too good, Faina. I want it to last and last."

I'm dragging in air as he quickens his pace, his hips slamming, his cock taking. Every thrust is deeper than the last. Every piston of his hips faster, marking me, claiming me. Skin against skin. Wet. Loud. Smacks.

"I can't—" It's all I manage before I start to come. And come. And fucking come because I swear my orgasm goes on and on—a vicious fire-breathing dragon that claws at my flesh and tears the muscle from my bones. I'm grinding and pushing and aching and begging, and I can't stop it. I don't *want* to stop it. It's the most mind-bending experience of my life.

And just when I think it's starting to ebb, Dex grabs me, his mouth back against mine, and he stills, growing rigid. His cock thickens, and then I feel it pulsing against the contractions of my pussy. Every grunt and groan and breath and word from him tickles my lips, all the while I feel him filling me up.

His mouth moves against mine, kissing me now, pulling me tighter into him, and then dragging me off the counter and onto the floor.

I can't help my laugh. "What are we doing?"

He laughs with me. "I can't stand. My legs are absolute jelly, but I couldn't leave you up there without me. I wanted a snuggle. I wanted to hold you against me."

He tucks me against his chest, holding me close and running his hands through my hair, and damn him. Damn him for being so perfect. For being the man I deserve. The one I've been seeking without knowing it all these years.

His cock is still half inside of me, even as wetness starts to pool between us.

"I'm leaking on you."

He groans, thrusting up, pushing himself back into me. "Better now?"

I giggle, and it makes him groan again, louder this time,

but the sound quickly dies as he props himself up and then stares at me.

"In my mind, I feel like a broken record. After every time I'm inside you, I think, wow, that was the best sex of my life. I'm thinking it again, only it's so much stronger. That wasn't just sex to me, Faina. Maybe I shouldn't say that, but it wasn't. I'm not sure what the right word for it is, but sex is too basic and clinical for what that was."

Before I can formulate any sort of a response, he kisses me, and that kiss turns into round two on the floor. After that, we both clean up, and I throw on pajamas because, despite his protests, I'm not eating dinner in only my bra and panties. Somehow the food isn't ruined, just cold, and after reheating it and watching Dex open a bottle of wine like a pro, we take our plates and sit in front of the fireplace instead of at the dining room table.

The only lights we have on are the Christmas tree that glows with its multicolored lights, and the fire, making it cozy and romantic.

It's perfect. So perfect.

"That wasn't you!" I gasp, trying not to choke on my mashed potatoes—my absolute favorite. Dex has had me laughing practically nonstop since we sat down.

He gives me a dubious look. "Princess, are you honestly questioning if I was the mastermind behind swapping the internet button with the shutdown button on our math teacher's computer to get us out of having to take our senior exams? I'm hurt, you didn't know it was me."

"It took him all class to finally figure out that's what happened. I thought the poor man was going to cry every time his computer shut down."

He grins deviously, "It was bloody fantastic. I don't think you could do that now on current computers."

"Likely not," I agree. "Shame. It was a great prank. I'm shocked you didn't try to take credit."

"And get suspended?" He shakes his head, making a tsking noise. "No thanks. My dad would have murdered me."

I lift my wine glass, rolling the crystal back and forth in my hands. "Do you remember when the power went out?"

He gives me a devilish grin, moving in closer to me. "You mean when you were in wellness?"

My eyes pop open wide. "Yes. But how did you know I was in wellness?"

He starts laughing. "You and Ava were both in wellness. It was the middle of the day on a Friday, and Will wanted alone time with Ava without having to sneak around parents." He looks down for a moment, and then slowly his head lifts until he's staring at me through his lashes. "I was keen to be around you a bit too, so I called in a favor to a bandmate who was also an electrician. He cut the power to the school for me."

I blink rapidly at him. "You did that to spend time with me?"

He gives me a boyish smile, almost shy, complete with dimples. "I took you out for lunch. Remember?"

I shake my head and then think deeper about it. "It was the four of us."

He raises an eyebrow. "Was it?"

My eyebrows slant together as the memory pieces back together. "We all had lunch together, and then—"

"And then we went to Will's house. He and Ava went off somewhere, and you and I went swimming."

"You didn't talk to me," I say as the memory plays through my head. "We swam together for about half an hour before your friends started showing up, and you didn't say much of anything."

He takes a sip of his wine. "You made me nervous."

I cackle. "Right. Dex Chapman nervous over a girl."

He shakes his head in protest. "I was. You asked me how I did on one of our English papers—"

"Othello."

"Right. That was the bloke. I hadn't read the book. Just watched the movie and didn't do well on the paper. I was embarrassed and didn't want you to know."

"Oh." I blink at him, at a bit of a loss on what to say.

He leans in and kisses my lips. "Your brain intimidated me, and your beauty tied my tongue." Another kiss. "Honestly, you were so much like Will, and I was so much like Ava, I often wondered how they matched up so well, and why he never went for you instead when you truly are nearly physically identical."

"Opposites attract?" I shrug.

"Must be, because I never felt a thing for Ava, and not simply because she was my best mate's girl. But you? I looked at you, and my heart raced, and my mind spun."

He's making my heart race and my mind spin right now. "I still can't believe that."

"Believe it, love. It's all true. You were my high school crush. My unicorn girl."

I raise an eyebrow, but those damn butterflies can't keep the girlish smile from my lips even as I say, "And all those girls you fooled around with?"

He gives me a crooked smile, rubbing the tip of his nose against mine. "I was a teenage boy. Sex was fun, and the girls were willing. I never dated any of them. Not seriously anyway."

"No, you were always too into your music. Ava, Will, and I snuck into that club a few times to watch you with your band. Even then, I think we all knew you were the real thing and would make it."

"It was do or die for me. I never considered anything else as an option. What about you? What made you go into marketing and PR?"

"I grew up in LA," I point out, as if that should make it obvious.

Dex is unimpressed. "That's why you went to Harvard and studied that?"

"I took a marketing class my freshman year, and it seemed interesting. I was going to be an English major and chemistry minor, and I had no clue what I wanted to do with either of those. My marketing professor told me I had a natural knack for seeing how a product could be marketable and to try doing the same for people. So I did both, and it was fun. Creative almost, because, as you know, sometimes you have to spin shit into sugar and make it smell and taste good."

He laughs. "Well, you've certainly done that with me. No one has mentioned my breakup with Elise since I got here, and even Elsie is staying quiet about it now because she was hired on to work for a large firm and doesn't want to bollocks it up."

"Well, now that you're in the clear with your label and endorsements, what's next for superstar, Dex Chapman?"

"Finish writing this album and then go into the studio to lay it down. After that, it's all promotions and tours and things to sell it."

I scrunch my nose. "Do you hate that side of the business?"

"The touring? Never. I love playing to a live audience. The schedule is grueling, but so worth it. I don't love interviews or guest appearances on talk shows. I never do well with those."

"You just need a better coach."

His lips glide against mine, and then he goes back to his food. "You mean like a PR coach with lovely blue eyes and hair of golden silk?"

I roll my eyes. "Nope. Definitely not what I mean."

"Ah, my beautiful little elf, if only I could convince you."

I turn away, going back to my own food as I stare up at the Christmas tree. I've loved helping him with his posts and comments. I've loved the excitement and flutter of being the one to help fix his image. But I don't love being the woman in

the spotlight, and I'm not sure what else comes from being with Dex.

"What did you use to do for Christmas with your parents?" I ask, changing the subject as I take a sip of my wine. He hasn't talked a lot about his family. I know he's an only child, and I remember his dad being sick when we were in high school. I believe he died shortly after we graduated, and he mentioned his mom passing a few months back.

He leans back against the couch, chewing as he thinks, his gaze cast out toward the dancing orange flames in the hearth. "When I was a boy and we were living in London, we'd eat dinner at a posh hotel with some of my dad's mates and business acquaintances." He turns to me. "It was miserable. I hated it. I had to wear an itchy suit and be on my best behavior. Once we moved to LA, it was parties. Same sort of deal to them though. Eventually, once I got old enough, I'd crash Will's Christmas. But after my dad died and Mum and I moved back to the UK, and I was starting to make some waves as a musician, Mum and I mostly hung in. We had our cook make us turkey and Christmas pudding with all the trimmings, and we'd drink and tell stories about my dad."

"You miss them." It's not a question, but he nods all the same. "I miss my parents too. Especially this time of year."

"I wasn't looking forward to Christmas this year. Knowing it would be my first after losing Mum. I have to say, this might be one of the best Christmases I've ever had." He leans in and kisses me softly, pulling back and licking his lips. "And meals for that matter. If your whole PR business doesn't work out, I might hire you to be my personal chef."

I roll my eyes again. "Har, har. I'd poison you within a week."

A smile lights his face, making his dimples come out. "I suppose it's a good thing our little adventure won't quite make it past that point."

I quirk an eyebrow. "I suppose so."

He leans forward, his smile now against my own. "You don't mean that, and you know I don't either. You're having as much fun with me as I am with you. Try and deny it, princess, but we're both caught in each other's webs. Struggling is futile."

## Chapter Twelve

Dex

"HAPPY CHRISTMAS," I whisper into Faina's neck sometime near dawn. Her small body is curled against mine, tucked under the heavy down quilt, bracing against the frigid morning air and the storm that blustered in last night. Outside the window, snow is whipping sideways in sheets of heavy white crystals.

I had a whole day planned for us, but with a foot or more of snow expected to fall just today, I don't think we'll be leaving. Honestly, I think I prefer it this way. Quiet. Snowed in. Just us.

What started off as a fling—a bit of fun—has quickly grown into so much more, but I have a feeling I'm the only one hanging out on that branch, and any moment, it could snap, and I'll plummet to my death. I'd question if this were a rebound. A transference of feelings, but my feelings for Elsie were all but naught when I caught her with that slimy bloke in our bed. The way I feel about Faina is more like muscle memory.

Like going years without swimming, but when someone tosses you into the pool, you automatically know what to do and how to do it.

"Mmmm," she hums, rolling and tucking herself in tighter against me. "Why do my limbs feel so heavy today?"

"Because they've been getting quite the workout."

"I guess I don't need sex lessons anymore?"

I grin, pressing my lips into her hair. "You know you never did, right? But whatever lessons we've had, you've passed with top marks."

Her head tilts, putting her face deeper into my neck, where she gives me a soft kiss right on my throat. My body sighs, so bloody content I can hardly stand it.

"Well, if that's true—the achiever in me loves that, by the way—I should go out and practice my newfound skills."

"Like fucking hell, you will." With a growl, I roll us until I'm on top of her and she's pinned beneath me, both of us cocooned by the blanket. I grind into the V between her legs, watching as her lips part when my hardening cock makes precise contact. "This is mine, Faina." *Grind.* "No man can have this." *Grind. Ever,* I want to say but don't.

And with my next grind, I slide inside her, punctuating my point until she cries out my name twice.

After our morning exercise, we make breakfast and coffee, and I start a fire in the fireplace. Wind howls past the house, but neither of us seems to mind as we turn on the telly and snuggle in under a blanket.

"I didn't get you anything," she declares, her voice forlorn, making me chuckle.

"What I ordered for you couldn't make it here in time. Evidently being in the mountains of Wyoming has its limitations. Too bad, too, it would have been lovely to unwrap it from your body."

"Are you sad we're not going to the spa and then out for fancy dinner?"

"Nah," I tell her, pulling her body tighter into mine. "This is perfect. I could spend every Christmas like this and be happy forever." The words come out light and off-the-cuff, but they hit me—and hit me hard. I mean, I knew I had feelings for Faina. I knew I wanted more time with her beyond this week—that one week wouldn't be enough. But the rightness of what I just said resonates deep within me, so deep I feel it in my bones. In my soul.

I wrote two songs last night in record time—pun intended—and both were about new adventures. About time not being on our side. About finding something new and wondering if it's real enough to keep.

Is that what I want with Faina?

To keep her? Beyond a fling or a few weeks of fun. And what would that entail? How would something like that ever work? Would she even consider that with me?

Thankfully she takes my comment as off-hand and doesn't press me. We watch holiday movies and eat leftovers, and I work on music while she reads and fiddles about on her laptop. She asks me to play for her, and I end up giving her a private concert, unable to stop because the look in her eyes when I sing to her makes my pulse race.

It isn't until a text comes in that I pause, setting my guitar down to pick up my phone.

"What's this?" I laugh.

"What you need to post on your social media."

"It's a video of me singing to you."

She nods, hopping out of her chair and skipping over to me. "Post it and wish everyone a Merry Christmas."

"But you're not in it."

She shakes her head. "I don't need to be. You're shirtless, only wearing flannel pajama pants, with a Christmas tree behind you on one side and snow out the window on the other. It's Christmas porn, and it will be the cherry on top of everything you've done this week."

I do as my lady commands and then toss my phone onto the sofa and take her in my arms. "You're magic." And I think I might be falling for you. I think I want all my Christmases to be yours. All my moments, actually.

I know I won't be able to let her go when this week is over.

But I have no clue how I'll convince her to stay.

"We should try the hot tub," I say, needing to clear all that away.

Her eyebrows shoot up. "The hot tub?" She glances past my shoulder to the storm outside.

"It'll be brilliant. It's somewhat covered by the overhang, and there's a gas fireplace out there we can turn on. The water will be warm, and we'll bring alcohol."

"Alcohol into a hot tub?"

"Sure. What else do we have to do?"

"Are we talking bathing suits?"

"I honestly don't think my bollocks could handle walking out there naked, so I'm going to say yes. For now," I amend because the idea of her naked in the hot tub... yeah, I'm definitely going to have to see that.

Ten minutes later, we're both in bathing suits, bathrobes, and bloody winter coats. We started the hot tub from inside as well as the gas fireplace because the owners of this rental are seriously clever and thought ahead.

Both of us watch the heavy billows of steam rising off the blue, bubbling water from our warm perch at the window.

"Why are we doing this again?" she questions.

"I honestly can't remember, but it sounded fun, and we're dressed for the occasion. Hold tight." I run back into the kitchen, grab the bottle of bourbon I bought, and return.

Faina eyes the bottle with a scrunched-up nose. "No glasses? Or ice?"

I laugh. "If you want bloody ice, just scoop up a handful of fucking snow. But now, it's straight from the bottle for us, princess. Rock star style."

"I'm not sure I'm groupie material," she admits.

"Aw love, we all have a bit of the groupie in us. Come on. It'll be fun. Or fucking awful, and we'll come back in and get in the bathtub upstairs to defrost."

She rolls her head around and shakes out her shoulders and hands. "Okay. I'm in. I'm ready. Let's do it."

Shit. I was sort of hoping she'd back out. "You go first."

She throws me a side-eye. "Wimp. You're supposed to be the badass of the two of us." Unlocking the back door, she slides the glass door open and immediately screeches. "Holy fuck, it's cold." But then she's shooting out the door, losing her winter coat and robe as she goes, before she flies up the three narrow steps of the deck and then practically dives head-first into the tub.

"Faina!"

"Ah! It's so cold, but the water is really warm, and it feels amazing. Come on!"

"Fuck!" I pace to my right and then left. I can do this. I can... not. "No, thanks. Enjoy the tub."

"Get in here! This was your idea, *badass*," she mocks, sinking down until just her head is above the water.

Dammit! She's right. Sucking in a breath, I jump out into the snow on the back deck, slamming the door shut behind me, and then sprinting toward the upper part where the hot tub is. "Why didn't we wear shoes?!"

"I don't know! We thought they would get in the way."

"I'm about to lose a bloody toe to frostbite."

"They'll thaw in the water. No! The robe!"

"Fuck!" I hiss, practically halfway into the water when I realize I'm still wearing my robe and rip it off, tossing it on the ledge of the deck. "Like it matters. It'll be soaked in the snow in no time. So much for this being covered. The wind is giving that part of the roof double middle fingers. How on earth will we get back inside? Our coats aren't near us, we have no shoes, and now our robes are lost to us."

Faina is cracking up, which of course makes me do the same, even as I bite out a slew of curses, sinking down into the boiling water.

"We didn't think this through," she snorts through her laughter.

"Clearly not. We should have put our coats and robes by the fire, worn goddamn boots, and then gotten in the water."

She shrugs, swimming over to me. "Too late. But if we die out here, we'll probably be too drunk to notice." She taps the bottle I've set on the ledge. "You saw this is a hundred and twelve proof, right?"

"I never check suck trivialities. Here." I yank the cork out and hand it to her. "First drink."

She shakes her head. "You go first."

"Ah, losing all your bravery already." I bring the bottle to my lips, and despite its massive alcohol content, it's smooth like a baby's arse. I take two large gulps and then hand it to her. "Here, love. Drink up."

She takes the bottle from me, and then I move over to the ledge, making sure only my head is above the surface, because yeah, it's seriously cold out. Twilight is masked by the deep shroud of clouds and heavy snow. Icy crystals sting my face, but other than that, with the fireplace hissing not even three feet from us and the world so quiet and dark, the mountains just barely visible in the distance, it's actually incredibly beautiful and peaceful.

Still...

"What the fuck were Ava and Will thinking?"

She sputters on her dainty sip, wiping her mouth with the fingers of her other hand. "I have no clue. They ski, but I'm starting to agree with your idea of Christmas in the tropics."

I bounce my eyebrows at her. "Coming over to the dark side, I see. I knew I'd corrupt you eventually. But truly, despite its beauty and peacefulness, could you ever live like this?" I ask, taking the bottle back from her and trying not to snicker too loudly at her grimace and shudder from the bourbon.

"No," she admits. "The town is adorable, and the mountains are stunning, but there is something about living in a city I love. What about you?"

"I've only ever lived in a city, so I'd have to agree." I take a few large gulps, already feeling the heat of the bourbon warming me from my belly upward. "Truth or dare?"

She laughs, rolling her eyes, even as she takes the bottle back from me and answers, "Truth."

"Wimp."

"So says the man who pushed me out the door first." She takes a small sip.

I won't go there. "Fine. What's a secret you've never told anyone?"

She blanches. "Yeesh. You could have started with an easier one."

I shake my head, snatching the bottle back from her and moving over to sit beside her. "Not my game."

"So I'm learning." She tucks herself in against me, and the hand not holding the bottle wraps around her, pulling her over me and tickling the skin on her side as air bubbles of warm water woosh around us. "Okay. Let me think. A secret I've never told anyone. I tell Ava pretty much everything, so this is even trickier." Then she laughs. "Actually, I have one you'll find amusing. Will kissed me once."

"What?" I stir beneath her, shifting her so I can see her face.

She laughs harder at my outraged expression. "He thought I was Ava. I was sitting outside under the oak tree at school waiting for her, but I was wearing one of Ava's shirts, and my hair was up when I usually wear it down, and suddenly his lips were on mine. I was so startled it took me a second to realize what the hell was going on, and when I shoved him back, he quickly realized his blunder and apologized profusely. He made me swear never to tell anyone, and I didn't because it was not something I ever wanted to think about again, and frankly, Ava would have been pissed even though it was an honest mistake."

I can't help but laugh with her. "You really don't have any demons hiding in your closet, do you?"

She rolls her eyes at me. "I don't know. You make me sound so…"

"Boring," I finish for her when she trails off.

"Ass." She splashes me. "Yes. You make me sound boring."

I lick a drop of water that's rolling down her neck and slide my hand down until I'm gripping her waist beneath the water. "You're not boring. You're just so deliciously sweet and pure, that's all. Nothing wrong with that, and truth be told, it's one of my favorite things about you."

She huffs, but she can't hide her smile. "Fine. Truth or dare?"

I want to say dare, but I'm afraid she'll send me out into the cold and snow, so I say, "Truth," instead.

"Wimp," she tosses back at me, making me smile against her neck as I kiss her skin.

"Definitely a wimp. You may be sweet and pure, but I already know there's a wicked side to you."

She wiggles against me, liking that description. "What's your biggest fear?"

"That's easy. Disappointing my fans and losing my musical mojo."

She sighs. "I get another one. That was too easy."

I pinch her side making her yelp. "That's not how this works. What's your relationship dealbreaker?" I ask.

She twists in front of me, lowering herself deeper into the water and staring up at me with clear, bright blue eyes, even in the waning darkness. "You didn't ask truth or dare."

"Now we're playing truth or truth, and if I want to dare

you to something, I'll just start taking from your body instead."

She moves over to me, her chest against mine and her head tilted back, her legs swiveling in the water, kicking out behind her. "That's easy," she parrots my words. "Cheating."

I grunt, rolling my eyes, and then take another sip from the bottle before handing it to her. "Other than cheating, princess. That's a given. For both of us, clearly."

"Lying, I guess. Or being with someone who doesn't see me. I don't want someone to want to change me. I want them to want me just as I am."

*As I do*, I think, but again, refrain from speaking my thoughts. For once.

I don't think Faina is ready to hear that I'm starting to believe she's the one I was always meant to end up with. At some point, I'll just have to come out and say it. I'll have to put my heart on the line and hope and pray she takes a chance with me.

But not yet. Not tonight.

"What about you?"

"Same. Most women want me for my money or fame or the fact that I'm a musician, since there is something about that to them. I want someone to want to be with me for me and for no other reason." Like her. She's rejected the notion of continuing this fling with me more than once. I've never had to work remotely this hard to try and make a woman mine before. And while the challenge and game are fun to a certain degree, the fear of losing makes anything but winning impossible.

I've never felt such a tormenting and blinding need to completely own someone physically and mentally as I do her. I want her heart. I want it as mine. And I need her to want to hold mine beside hers as well.

I don't want her for what she can do to help my career,

and I don't want her simply because she's fantastic in bed. I want *her*. All of her.

I love making her smile and laugh. I love seeing how she pushes herself past her comfort zone and is trying to not just embrace life but take it by the bollocks and make it her own. I love getting to know all the little things about her, things I never knew in all the time I knew her.

In turn, I love who I am when I'm with her. I love how she makes me feel and the way she sees past all that I am to the world. She sees the man I am inside.

She's not someone I can give up.

Not when I'm discovering that there isn't anything about her that I don't already love.

"Come here," I whisper, my voice strangled and desperate as I drag her face up and her lips to mine. She tastes like bourbon and that combined with her sweet body against mine and the water and the snow and fucking Christmas and all this bourbon sloshing in my belly, I'm drugged.

But more than that, I'm consumed.

And quite frankly, in love.

## Chapter Thirteen

Faina

THE WEEK between Christmas and New Year's passes us by in a blur. We tried skiing, but after one lesson and me practically taking down the J-bar lift thing, both of us called it quits. It was decided that we are much safer and happier on two feet instead of two sticks.

That didn't stop us from ice skating and falling all over the place though, much to the amusement of other skaters who were quick to take photos and videos and post them everywhere. It's been great for Dex and even for me because, as Dex promised, I've already started receiving job offers.

Only, I've already made a decision.

I'm going to do this on my own. I'm going to start my own PR and marketing company. I'm just not sure where or how, but that can all be figured out later. I'm excited about it and have already started looking into business names and logos and things of that nature.

But amidst that excitement, a heaviness is eating me alive.

Tonight is New Year's Eve, and tomorrow is New Year's Day, and then we leave on the second of January. That's it. The rental is gone, and this trip is over, and so is my holiday fling with Dex.

We haven't talked about it again since he mentioned extending this to another location and me shooting it down. I'm not regretting that decision either, but that doesn't mean I want this to end. Just the thought of us going our separate ways wrecks me with a grief so powerful it steals the oxygen from my lungs.

But what alternative do I have?

Move to London after only being with a man for ten days? And we're not even actually together. Nor has he asked me to do that. We're both coming out of not-so-great relationships, and I know he doesn't want to dive into another.

But I can't be a fling anymore.

A woman he passes the time with between the sheets while playing at more for the world. When we're alone, it feels all too real. But it's not. It's sex without the possibility of love, and I can't do that with him. I already feel too much. I already pine for more.

Which is why this has to end. I broke my rule, and I caught feelings—big, fat feelings—and it sucks. But it's also been the best time of my life, and I have no regrets, despite the imminent heartbreak headed my way.

Dex moved our Christmas dinner to tonight. Evidently, New Year's is a big deal here. They have a glowstick and a torchlight parade down the mountain that makes the whole thing look like it's illuminated by fire, and then fireworks at midnight. I'll admit, I've never been a huge New Year's person, but I'm excited for tonight.

Especially as I slip into the dress Dex bought me. It's red and long, but with a plunging neckline and a monster slit up the side that makes it so I can't wear the lingerie that finally arrived. The dress is downright sexy and hits my curves in every place it should.

By the time I exit the upstairs bathroom—since I kicked Dex out and made him use the one downstairs—I feel like a siren. Red lipstick paints my lips, and black liquid liner streaks my upper lids. My hair is down in thick, glossy waves that bounce around me as I walk down the stairs, my heels clicking on the hardwood floors as I do.

Dex is facing the Christmas tree, his back to me, his shoulders slightly hunched, and a hand on his hip as if he's deep in thought, but when he hears me coming, he swivels around and then freezes on the spot. His eyes widen and his lips part, a flush slowly growing on the upper part of his cheeks as his bottle-green eyes dilate into twin pools of lust.

He doesn't look so bad either. In fact, he's downright delectable in a sharp, classic black tuxedo with a white shirt and black bowtie. His longish on top sandy-blond hair is brushed back, making his smooth face and sharp jawline more pronounced.

"Good evening, Mr. Chapman."

He opens and closes his mouth, but no sound comes out, and that seems to make him laugh. "You're so stunning, I can hardly form words." He shakes his head, running his thumb along his lips. "Christ, Faina. You're a goddess," he rasps instead of returning my greeting. He takes a step toward me, his eyes glued to every inch of me as they do one sweep after another. "Can't we stay in instead?"

"No way," I tell him, reaching the bottom of the stairs and crossing the room until my fingers twine with his. "You promised me a fancy dinner."

His free hand slides into the slit at my thigh and glides up and then back, cupping and squeezing my ass, and then he continues searching, only he's not going to find what he's looking for. And when he realizes I'm not wearing anything beneath my dress, he presses himself against me, making me feel how hard he is for me.

"Where are the items I bought you?"

"Unable to be worn with this dress without them showing through."

His eyes blaze. "So you're naked under this?"

"You'll have to find out. Later."

Only that answer doesn't satisfy him, and that hand on my ass moves to my front until he's cupping my mound, pressing his fingers firmly against my lips, and putting pressure on my clit as his fingertips skim my wet opening.

He groans, his forehead dropping to mine. "You're torturing me." He thrusts his hard cock into my hip. "Please, please, let me eat you now."

"Not a chance." But even as I say it, my core disagrees and clenches, seeking more of his fingers. He feels it and groans again, his breathing ragged.

"Most gorgeous woman I've ever seen, and she makes me wait even when she wants it just as badly."

"It'll only make this better," I promise as I slide his hand away.

He cocks an eyebrow. "Oh, so now who's the teacher?"

I smirk, giving him a wink. "I learned from the best. Let's go."

We slip on our winter coats, and then he opens the door for me, followed by the passenger door of the car. Twenty minutes later, we're pulling up in front of the Four Seasons, the entrance lined with people. It isn't until the valet opens the door for us and we're bombarded by flashing lights and shouts that we realize what's happening.

"Dex! Dex, over here. Is it true that you and Faina are now engaged?" "Dex, what do you have to say about the reports that Elsie was caught cheating on the man she left you for?" "Faina, are you moving to London to be with Dex?" "Is it true you're secretly pregnant with his child?"

Dex races around the car and throws his arm around my shoulders, tucking me into his side to shield me from their cameras, and then pushes us through toward the entrance of the hotel. We're quickly swallowed by the revolving door, and then there's a woman in a sharp suit there to greet us.

"Mr. Chapman, I'm so very sorry. They arrived moments before you did. We were not alerted to their presence in time to warn you."

Dex is ready to burn down the world as he regards her with a steady look. "Get. Them. Out. Of. Here. Now."

"Yes, sir. We're working on it now. Again, I'm so sorry. We have the library all set up for you as you requested. It's this way." She leads us deeper into the hotel, which is rustic and beautiful, but I can't focus on any of that. Dex grips my hand, but it's not enough for him. He's holding me close, his body vibrating with anger, and the moment we're led into the library and the doors are shut behind us, he's all over me.

"Are you okay?" he asks, his voice stricken. "I'm so sorry. I have no idea how they found us or knew we'd be here now."

"I'm fine," I tell him, trying to calm him down by putting my hand on his flushed face. "It was… a lot. But I'm fine."

"Faina." He tears away from me, running a hand through his hair as he paces toward the roaring fire and then back. "They're going to be all over us now that they're in town."

"I know."

"No, baby, I don't think you do."

My chest quakes at what he's intimating. And the fact that this is the first time he's called me baby. "What are you saying, Dex?" I need him to spell it out for me.

"I'm saying maybe we should leave early."

Genuine regret lines his features, and I turn away from him, needing to hide the sudden rush of agony that rips through me. One small blip, and he's ending this. Just like that. A man who is used to the press. If anyone should want to run from this, it's me, but the thought never even occurred to me.

Still, if I'm already feeling this way at the notion of it ending, perhaps doing it sooner rather than later is better. Better for my heart. Better for my head. Better for my life that he's already thrown into an uproar.

"I suppose you're right. Maybe leaving early is the prudent thing to do. It was going to end in forty-eight hours anyway," I remark, walking over toward the table that's set with white linens and beautiful crystal glasses. There's a chilled bottle of champagne sitting in an ice bucket, and I pull it out, going about pulling off the foil so I can get to the cork.

"What?" Dex barks when the door opens, and a server enters carrying a tray with two dishes on it as well as a bread bowl, and thank God for that. Carbs will save the day.

"Miss, let me help you with that."

The waiter sets the tray down on the side table and places the plates on top of the empty place settings and then comes to retrieve the bottle from me. I'm sure I'm the first guest to ever attempt to open their own champagne here, but I don't care. He finishes the job I started and then, with a loud *pop*, opens the bottle and pours two glasses.

"For you." He hands one to me, and I gratefully take it, downing half of it without waiting for a toast or the guy to even give us privacy. Thankfully he doesn't comment and can clearly read a situation for what it is. "I'll let you enjoy your amuse-bouche and be back in a bit."

Excusing himself, I finish off the glass and pour myself a second one.

"What's going on here, Faina? Why are you drinking like that and talking about ending this when all I said was that we should leave early?"

I turn on him to find him right in front of me, and I stagger back a step, needing the space. "Because from my understanding, we end when this ends, and I just didn't expect you to want to run out on it the first chance you got."

He shakes his head, anger coiling up his face. "That's not how I meant it, and it sure as hell is not what I want."

"You're not making sense, Dex. You say you want to go, but I'm not sure what you're expecting from me. What happens to me when this all ends? The world will hate me. They'll say I broke your heart."

He sighs plaintively. "I won't let that happen. I won't."

"It won't matter," I cry. "You didn't cheat on Elsie, and yet one video, a few sad words from her, and that was all it took for the court of public opinion to rule you guilty. They were asking if we were engaged. If I was pregnant. It's a mess. So much more than a few simple pictures."

His hard eyes are all over me, his expression stoic, so unlike him. "I still don't see why this has to end. Even if our holiday does."

I shake my head, turning that over in my mind for a moment. "How can it not? We live on different continents."

Urgently, he advances, getting right up in my face, his hands coming to my waist. "But we don't have to, Faina. That's what I was going to suggest." He licks his lips nervously. "Actually, I was going to bring it up tonight anyway, just not like this. What if you came home with me to London."

"Dex—"

"No," he cuts my protest off, urgently grabbing my shoulders. "Just listen. Why can't we keep this going? Why can't we see where it takes us?"

"See where it takes us? You're talking about me moving in with you? About me moving to a foreign country. We've been fooling around for just over a week."

He shakes his head in warning, practically growling at that. "Don't do that. Don't dismiss this. I've known you practically my entire life. You're not new to me, and neither is the way I feel about you." He pulls away from me, pacing in an agitated circle before rounding back on me. "Fine. You're not ready to move in with me. I get it. It's a huge ask. But let's give this some more time. I can stay here in the States. Or we can go someplace else. Somewhere we can be together without the world interfering."

My eyes burn with tears as my throat closes up on me. "I already told you I can't location jump with you." I blow out a breath. "You wanted the world involved, and now it is. What did you think would happen with all this?" I pan my hand out toward the entrance of the hotel. "We're all over the internet. Millions of views on your posts alone. I tried not to think about it because we were still in this bubble and that all felt so far away, so removed, but now it's here, and that doesn't go away simply because you've changed your mind and no longer want it. If we stay together, it follows us."

He grunts and looks toward the fire. "I don't want it to end. Ever."

I push out a breath. "I don't want it to end either. But I'm not sure what our alternative is."

His gaze slingshots back to mine, desperate and intense. "The alternative is we don't throw this away. We fight for it. We don't wash our hands of it simply because the logistics are tough and not as we'd like them to be."

I start to argue with him, but he quickly cuts me off, not letting me get a word in.

His hand cups my jaw, his eyes right in front of mine, fierce and unrelenting. "Do me a favor. Close your eyes and try to imagine the rest of your life. Try to imagine yourself with someone else. Someone better. Do it," he demands sharply, and my eyes snap shut, my body trembling as tears start to leak. "Do you see him?"

I make a strangled noise, my eyes pinching tighter.

"You don't, do you? You can't see anyone else because there is no one better for you than I am." His hands press in on me, forcing my eyes back open, forcing me to stare straight into his. "You talked about wanting to be loved for who you are. For not wanting someone to want to change you. I fucking love you, Faina, and there is nothing about you that I would ever change. To me, you are perfect. To me, you are everything I could ever want. You can walk away and try to find a different version of your life, but it'll never be as good as the version where we're together. You only die once, Faina. How do you want to live?"

# Chapter Fourteen

Dex

TEARS LEAK one after the other from her eyes, despair woven through her every feature. She's about to break my heart, and I'm unprepared for the blow. She's right about everything she said. I wanted the world's eyes on us, and I got it, but it came at a price I'm no longer willing to pay. They'll move on eventually. They always do.

But Faina doesn't see that—it's not a world she's experienced before—and trying to fall in love and start something real is nearly impossible when both people aren't invested and willing to brave the storm.

"I don't want to be afraid anymore," she whispers. "I don't want…" Her eyes flash. "I don't want to leave here and lose everything we've found in each other this week. I've never had this. Not anything remotely close. But… how? Tell me how that doesn't happen."

My hands meet my hips, my eyes dropping to the floor before they slowly rise to hers. "What is it you want me to do,

Faina? How can I show you that I want this with you? That I'm willing to fight and do what it takes to make you love me and keep you as mine?"

She sets her glass down. "I don't know. But I think it's too late now. I think this is all about to blow up in our faces."

"Like bloody hell it is," I grab her arm, startling her. "Come with me."

"What?"

"Come. With. Me. I'm going to take care of this once and for all, and then you'll know."

I give her a solid jerk, and then suddenly we're leaving the library and marching back down toward the exit.

"Dex! What are you doing?" People are staring at us, whispering at the enraged rock star dragging his girlfriend toward the exit of one of the most posh hotels in the world. But right now, I don't give a toss.

"Making a formal announcement," I tell her. "Since I have no PR agent at present, I am my own man."

"This isn't smart," she hisses, but I'm undeterred.

I told Faina I loved her, but now I need to prove it because my girl still isn't sold. And why should she be? Men have told her that and lied through their teeth. They've used her for their own selfish needs—myself included in this—and she needs—*deserves*—more.

My head whips back around. "I'm going to make a statement, and then you and I are going to talk and eat back up in that library because it's bloody fucking cold out here. Are you ready?"

"Ready? No! No, I'm not ready. Why are you doing this?"

I swoosh my arm around her waist and drag her to my chest. "Because sometimes the only way a man can prove himself to the woman he loves is through a grand gesture." I smack a kiss to her lips, release her, and then march outside, leaving her behind inside the hotel because I don't want her to be cold, and this is something I need to do. "And this is all I've got right now," I murmur to myself as the icy wind hits my face.

I think I've officially gone insane.

Everything we're ever taught or told as celebrities is about to go straight out the window. Never speak directly to the press. Always schedule interviews if necessary. You need to be the one to control the narrative, not them.

Whelp, I have to prove to Faina that I don't want this to end, and I have to prove to her that the world won't hate her and that we can be together. I have to prove my love. So here goes nothing.

I march out into absolutely frigid air, Faina hovering by the door, unsure of my motives. It's a stretch. I know it is.

She might be looking for an excuse to get rid of me, but in my gut, I don't think that's the case. I think my good little princess is just scared. She doesn't do well when pushed, and I plan to push her—and push her as far as I can. Starting now.

Lights flash like fireworks in my eyes as I approach the wrangling of arseholes, otherwise known as tabloid paparazzi. My name, along with dozens of questions, shoot passed their lips, but I'm not having it. I will not be baited. Instead, I plan to use them. And then get the fuck back inside because my toes and fingers are already numb.

I hold up my hand, quieting them down. "Since you all crashed my holiday, I felt I should set a few things straight once and for all. First, I never cheated on Elsie. Ever. That video she felt the need to post that I stayed quiet on was taken months ago, and she was the one filming it. She was very much an equal and active participant. Second, the bloke's nose I broke was her lover's, and I broke it after finding them together in my bed. But, truthfully, I have to thank her for that. Because if it wasn't for her philandering ways, I'd never have reunited with Faina, and let me tell you, Faina is incredible. She's everything to me, and I know you're all here to get photographs of me with her. So here's my deal to you. You may snap a picture or two and use it how, you'd like and ask a few questions, but then you bugger off and leave us be. It's new between us, and while new doesn't always turn into forever, I'm hoping this one gets the chance to test that. Do we have a deal?"

And because they're arseholes, they snap a dozen more pictures and bark out a hundred more questions, but again, I stop them.

"Do we have a deal? If not, Faina and I will hide and do everything in our power to make your jobs and lives far more difficult. If you scare her off or slander her name in any way, I will not only make your lives more difficult, I will destroy them. It's now or never, I promise you that."

For once in their pesky lives, they're silent, and while I likely shouldn't have threatened them—you can blame my lack of proper PR to guide me—it seems to have worked. Speaking of proper PR, I turn and watch as Faina stands in the doorway of the hotel, arms wrapped protectively around her body, eyes wary and helpless, and my stomach flips over on itself.

What if she doesn't do this with me?

I die ten thousand deaths in the span of two seconds before she pushes away from the door, and saunters in my direction, a coy smile curling up her lips as she does. She reaches me and then slides in beside me and takes charge in a way that makes my cock instantly harden despite the sub-artic temperatures.

Speaking of, I shuck out of my jacket and drape it over her shoulders, and she glances up quickly, giving me a gleaming smile before it just as quickly evaporates and she turns back to the press, all business and sexy as fuck.

"Good evening, ladies and gentlemen, and Happy New

Year. Despite what Dex just claimed, he will not be answering any questions or making any further statements. I will allow a few pictures, but that's it, and after that, we kindly ask that you respect our need for privacy."

She turns to me and gives me a Hollywood smile that the cameras start eating up. I note she doesn't kiss me, and I don't push it because I still don't know where we are.

"Does this make you my new PR rep, Miss Spencer?" I murmur through my teeth so only she can hear me.

"Don't get ahead of yourself, Mr. Chapman."

"Me?" I quip. "Always."

After that, my queen—she's been upgraded from princess after that fierce move—says we're all done. The press isn't thrilled about that at all, especially since I didn't answer any questions, but whatever. They weren't going to leave us alone as it was, no matter what I made them promise.

They're paparazzi.

It wasn't about them as much as telling them and the world what Faina means to me.

And since I am but her servant, I follow after her, rubbing her arms over my jacket to warm her up. Briskly, we walk back to the library, ignoring everyone standing around the lobby gawking madly at us, and when we enter, we immediately head for the fire that is thankfully blazing high.

She turns on me. "You're crazy."

"I thought you already knew that about me."

She smiles, nibbling on her lip a bit to try and hide it. "I can't believe you did that."

I pivot to face her, stepping into her, so she's forced to crane her neck to meet my eyes. "There isn't anything I wouldn't do to prove how much I love you."

"Alright. I just have one more thing to ask of you."

I swallow thickly and nod for her to continue. "Anything."

"Tell me how we turn a holiday fling into forever?"

My answer is immediate. It's easy. Probably because unbridled joy is expanding in my chest like a balloon, and I feel as though I'm about to float right out of his room. I crash my lips to hers and kiss her with everything I've got, walking her back until I've got her pinned to the wall.

I continue to kiss her until we're both breathless. "This is how we turn a holiday fling into forever. By never letting go. By always kissing and making up instead of fighting and splitting up. I want to be with you. Wherever you are. I don't want long-distance, Faina. And I don't want to take this slow and see how it all sorts out. I don't think I can do that with you. Tell me what you need for this to happen, and I'll do it."

Breathlessly, she stares up at me, her eyes glittering. "I want to start my own company. That said, I don't know if I can work for you, though you certainly need help controlling your mouth."

I laugh. "I think if anything, I'll work for you. I might also beg you since you're the only one who can keep me in line. But I can help you with whatever you need to get yourself started."

"I've never lived in London," she says, her voice cautious.

I search her eyes. "Where were you thinking of moving to?"

"LA."

I groan, my forehead falling against hers. "I bloody hate LA."

She laughs. "Me too. But it's where Ava is."

"No. Ava is all over and rarely in LA. They're only there now because Will is sick. New York?"

"You live in London," she counters.

"And I'm offering New York with you."

She sags back against the wall, breathing heavily, her mind running circuits. "Just like that, you'll move to America? To New York?"

"For you? Yes. Hell, if you really pushed it, I'd even move back to LA."

Her hands come up, her fingers gliding along my jaw. She stares at my mouth, and then her eyes bounce up to mine. "I could try London. If you're willing to move to New York or even LA, if I pushed it, I could try London for you first, and we'll see how it goes."

I attack her, right here against the wall, my hand diving up her dress, needing to feel her bare flesh against my palm. "I love you," I whisper against her lips. "I said fuck the first time I told you, and a man should never tell the woman he loves that he loves her for the first time by using the word fuck."

She laughs into me. "I... I think I love you too. I think that's what all this is. This swirling, giddy, I never want to let you go feeling. But this is crazy, right? I mean, who does this? Who plans forever with someone after only ten days?"

I drag my thumbs across her cheeks, staring straight into her eyes. "Us. We do." I give her the smile that never fails to dazzle her. "Will said it for me the other day. I've been obsessed with you since I learned all the fun that can be had by playing with my dick while thinking of you. As crude as that is, it's true. It's always been you, Faina. And it always will be."

My mouth devours hers again, my hand sliding into the slit on her thigh, and then up, up, until I find her slick pussy.

"Always so fucking wet for me."

"Mmmm," she hums, only for the sound to turn into a gasp as I slide two fingers inside her.

"I love this dress. I love that you're not wearing anything beneath it. It's the ultimate tease." My other hand tears down the shoulder, revealing one perfect breast for my mouth to lick and suck.

"Dex, we can't do this here."

"Why not? If I want to drop to my knees and eat you for dinner instead, tell me why I can't."

"Because any second, someone could walk in," she moans as I pump up into her till I'm knuckle deep.

"I can make you come quickly," I murmur against her nipple, blowing cold air on it and making her shiver.

"Dex!" She grasps onto my tuxedo jacket. "Stop."

"First you come, then I stop."

"Ah!" I turn my wrist and up my pace, hitting her front wall and rubbing her clit at the same time. I shift her dress back into place, covering her breast, because she's right, anyone could walk in, and then I swallow down her moans and cries and even protests. I shift so that if the door opens, the only thing they'll see is the back of me and not her.

And then I go to town, fucking her hard and fast with my fingers.

"If you're mine, I can make you come wherever and whenever I want, and you will love every minute of it while trusting me that I'd never compromise you. Come on, Queen, give me all your sweet cum."

Her hand fists my shirt, and then she's shuddering and shaking into her release.

"Mine," I whisper against her lips. "Mine, Faina. All mine. No one else's. Your heart. Your body. Your mind. Your soul. All fucking mine."

"Yes," she cries, swallowing her gasps. "Yours."

I slide my fingers out of her and then straight into my mouth so I can taste her orgasm. The way I burn for every piece of this woman is like nothing else. Using my other hand, I smooth her dress, readjusting her until she's perfect once more.

The door to the room opens not even two seconds later, and the waiter returns, taking us in as we're pressed against the wall. Faina's face flames, but I can't help my laugh, especially as he immediately turns red. He goes to retreat, but before the poor chap can excuse himself, I wave him in.

"Sorry, mate. We're going to eat now. I have to feed my lovely queen here, or she'll turn into a pumpkin sometime around midnight."

Faina smacks my arm, but we're both laughing too hard to sell it. I take her hand and lead her back to the table, helping her into her seat.

"Feel free to pour those glasses high," I tell the man. "We've got plenty to celebrate."

# Epilogue

Dex

ONE YEAR later

FAINA THINKS I'm going to propose to her tonight. Actually, she's thought that nearly every day this week. Today is Christmas, and this year, instead of being trapped in the snow, we're on an island in the Bahamas. A private island. An island where the only way on or off is by boat or helicopter, so there's no chance of the press or the outside world getting a piece of us.

"Are you doing it today?" Will asks, taking a sip of his margarita, one arm casually tossed behind his head as he stares out toward the edge of the water where Faina and Ava are standing and chatting.

"Not a chance. She's expecting it."

"Does she know yet?"

I tilt my head in his direction, reluctantly tearing my gaze away from my girl in her hot pink bikini. "Know what?"

"That you've got the ring on you at all times?"

I shrug and turn back to her. "Probably. She's tenacious that way, but if she's seen it, she hasn't let on yet."

"Do you remember when I proposed to Ava?" he asks, and I choke on my sip of margarita, because yes, I do remember that.

"You mean when you told her you weren't going to be in Vegas and then showed up anyway, crashed her birthday dinner with her sister, and then she threw up all over the side-walk after you got down on one knee in front of the fountain?"

He smiles. "Yeah. You're forgetting the part where a homeless man ran over and stole the bottle of champagne I had, but it was perfect. She didn't expect it."

"I think I'm missing your point here, mate."

"The element of surprise is a good thing. She thinks you're doing it tonight at Christmas dinner. I overheard her telling Ava that you were either going to propose tonight or on New Year's. So instead, you should go and do it now when she's not expecting it."

It's a thought.

"Or perhaps I should wait and do it on the opening night of my concert in two weeks. Really throw her off."

He raises his sunglasses and gives me a stink eye. "Do you know Faina at all? Somehow, I don't think proposing to her in front of seventy thousand screaming fans is the fairy tale way she had in mind."

"True. But it's not very romantic to just walk up to her, shove Ava out of the way, and then drop down onto one knee." Is it? I'm honestly not sure now because he does have a point about doing the unexpected.

This past year with Faina has been a dream. She moved to London with me, but I ended up selling my flat almost imme-diately. I didn't want her moving into the place where Elsie and I had lived. I wanted a place that would be only ours, so after finding and purchasing a new place, we moved in together.

I buckled down and wrote and recorded an album in record time, and six months ago, it was released, hitting number one on the charts. Six of the fourteen songs on the album stayed in the top ten for months. It's by far been my bestselling album of all time, and after the new year, I'm set to go on a three-month tour across the US and Europe.

Faina plans to join me here and there, but her agency has been growing like a weed. At first, it was just her with me— yes, I convinced her to take me on—as her first and only client. But that didn't last long. Within months, she had more clients than she could manage on her own and now has five full-time employees managing all the people and companies her business represents.

It'll be impossible not being with her all the time, which is why I want my ring on her finger so she knows my heart and body will never stray. Not that we have trust issues. Oddly enough, for two people who have been cheated on, neither of us seems to worry about that from the other. Maybe it's *because* we were both cheated on, but the way we trust one another isn't something I ever imagined I'd have with anyone.

"How's this? How about I go and snatch Ava under the pretense of taking a sexy walk, and you do it then?"

"A sexy walk?" I parrot.

"Yeah. You know. A walk where I take her somewhere and we fuck."

"Right." I rub my hand across my smiling lips. This is why Will will forever be my best mate. "Sounds like a plan. Let's do it."

He shoots upright in surprise. "You're serious? I was kidding."

I turn on him. "What do you mean you were kidding? It was your idea to propose now so she doesn't know it's coming."

"Fuck! Ava is going to kill me."

"What the bloody hell are you going on about?"

He runs a hand through his hair and sets his glass down on the small table between our chaises. "I promised her we could watch when you finally proposed."

I shake my head. "No way."

"Yes, way."

"I thought you were trying to get your wife pregnant. How do you intend to do that if you don't take her on your sexy walk?"

He grunts. "Fine. You're right. But you can't tell her it was my idea that you proposed, and you can't tell her I knew anything about it."

"Deal."

"Good." We both stand, and he smacks my shoulder, giving me a lazy smile. "Good luck, man. I'm super fucking excited for you. Marrying a Spencer girl is not for the faint of heart. It takes balls and luck and learning the divine art of groveling."

"Actually, mate, all I have to do is smile at my queen, and she's putty in my hands."

He scoffs. "I think you have that the other way around."

No denying that.

We make our way across the soft, powdery white sand toward our women, who are laughing about something or another. "Ava, Will says it's time to try and get you pregnant."

"Dick." Will smacks my shoulder. "You can't say that?"

I turn, staring at him bewilderedly. "Why ever not?"

"Because it's not sexy," he tells me all huffy like a little girl. "It's supposed to be a *sexy* walk."

"I thought sexy was just your prissy way of saying sex."

Ava and Faina are watching us, both with amusement dancing in their eyes.

"Christ." Will's hands meet his hips. "Faina, what on earth do you see in this guy?"

She shrugs, and I reach out and swat her ass, making her yelp. "Nice try, queen. You're totally gone on me."

"So, a sex walk or a sexy walk?" Ava asks, stepping into Will seductively. "Because we didn't do it this morning, and any day now, I'm supposed to be ovulating."

He grabs her hip, sliding his hand around to her ass. "I'll take either if it means I get to knock you up."

"So romantic," I tease, and he flips me off. "Yeah, you're welcome. Cheers, mate. Good luck." But then they're finally leaving us, and it's just me and Faina and my nerves that have taken on a life of their own.

"Crazy to think that they could make an actual baby right now."

"Yes. And sort of disturbing. I never want to picture your sister and Will having sex."

She laughs, sliding up against me and wrapping her arms around my neck. "What about us having sex?"

I grin down at my little elf. "That I'm always up for." I lean down and kiss her sweet, pillowy lips. "Admit it, this is far better than the freezing cold and feet of snow."

"Definitely. Though I do miss that gondola ride."

I shudder. "Never again, love. Never again."

I take her hand and walk us a bit deeper into the blue-green water, marveling at how I can see clearly to the sand beneath. The sun is high in the bright, cloudless sky, and the most perfect breeze kicks up off the water, rustling our hair.

"This might be my new favorite vacation spot."

"I never took a lot of vacations," she admits. "I was always too busy saving."

"Good. I like spoiling you. I like the idea that I can take you all over the world, and it will be your first time experiencing it all."

She tucks her head against my arm and sighs. A happy fucking sigh, and I feel like this is my moment. My heart races in my chest, thrumming blood through my ear and making my hands tremble as I reach into my pocket to retrieve the diamond I've carried on me so she wouldn't find it in my luggage.

"Fai," I start, only to have to clear my throat as emotion rolls over me.

"Hmmm?" she murmurs absently as waves lap at our legs and seagulls squawk in the distance.

"Happy Christmas."

She giggles lightly and peeks up at me, squinting through the sun since she's not wearing her sunglasses. "Merry Christmas."

I push my frames up onto my head and stare down at her. God, she's so lovely. So perfect and gorgeous and mine. I'm so lucky. So bloody lucky, and I need to make her mine forever. Hell, I want to take her on sex walks and put a baby in her belly. I want everything with her. Always.

Starting now.

With that thought in my head, my hand clasps the ring in my pocket, and I turn toward her, smiling like a goddamn fool because I can't stop myself.

"Do you know how much I love you?"

She places her hand on my chest over my thrashing heart. "Hopefully as much as I love you."

"More," I tell her. "I love you more. I'll always love you more. I never knew... I never knew it could be like this with anyone, but it is with you."

I slide my hand from my pocket and start to lower myself when something large slithers past my leg in the water making me jump, and the ring slips from my hand and into the water.

"Fuck!" I bellow, practically pushing Faina away so I can search the water for the ring.

"What? What is it?" she cries frantically, trying to come back at me because clearly she thinks I'm hurt or something is terribly wrong, which it is.

"I dropped the ring."

"The ring?" she snaps. "What ring?"

I give her an unimpressed look and then return to the water, searching everywhere for it. "Your engagement ring, Faina. Will suggested that I propose to you now when you're not expecting it, and I agreed, and now I've gone and dropped the bloody ring in the sodding ocean."

"You what?!" she shrieks, starting to search along with me. "Who brings a loose ring into the ocean to propose?"

"I don't know. I was trying to be bloody romantic. Clearly, I didn't think it through or expect a fucking blue whale to come out of nowhere and startle me half to death."

"A blue whale?" She starts laughing.

I throw her a glare. "It's not funny." Only now my lips are twitching too, because yeah, it's not funny at all, yet somehow, it strangely is. I groan and sigh. "It's hopeless. We'll never find it."

"I'm sure it was beautiful," she says, her lips still curled up at the edges.

"It was. I raided His Majesty's jewels from the Tower of London. Stole the biggest one I could find."

"Good thing we're here then where they can't catch you."

I move in to kiss her when she suddenly plows past me, her elbow catching me in the side as she shoots through the air and splashes down into the ocean, immediately going under.

"What in the almighty fuck?" I yell, ignoring my smarting ribs as I dive for her, only for her to emerge a second later, her hand held victoriously in the air, a triumphant smile spread across her face.

"I got it!"

"You do?!" I shout, lifting her out of the water until she's standing, her body and hair dripping water everywhere.

"That or I found someone else's engagement ring."

I belt out a laugh as I try to open her palm, but she just shakes her head and runs toward the beach, kicking water every which way as she goes.

"No way!" she tells me. "We're not making that mistake twice."

I follow after her, feeling nothing short of dejected. "This was the worst proposal in the history of the world," I grumble, kicking sand. She continues all the way until she's left the beach entirely and is on the stone hardscape of the pool.

"Well, it wasn't technically a proposal since you didn't ask anything," she notes, going under the shaded area and taking a seat.

I fall into the seat across from her, running my hand across my face and back through my hair. I shrug. "You're right. I didn't get that part right either."

But then she shocks me by getting down onto her knees in front of me, her closed fist resting on my thighs as she gazes up at me. "I love you," she says softly. "I love you so much. This last year has been the greatest whirlwind of my life, and something tells me that every day with you always will be. But more than that, I always want to make you smile and not frown, happy and not sad. I want to see and experience the world through your eyes. I want you to serenade me when you're in the shower, and I want to make you your grand English breakfast every Sunday. So what do you say? Will you marry me?"

She opens her hand and holds the diamond ring up at me, proposing to me.

"Will I marry you?"

She shrugs, but there is no hiding the love in her eyes or the joyful conviction in her smile. "I figured you might say yes since you bought the ring for me and all."

I laugh. "Of course, I'll marry you, queen." I shake my head.

That's not how this was supposed to go. Not at all.

I'm going to propose again to her. And this time, I'll get it right. Until then, I lift her off the ground and drop her right on my lap, and I kiss the hell out of her, taking the ring and sliding it right onto her finger.

"Will you marry me?" I ask against her lips.

"Yes," she breathes. "But remember, I asked you first."

I bite her shoulder, making her squeal and shove at me. "One-upper." I trickle kisses along her neck. "I love you," I murmur into her sun-kissed skin. "So much."

Her arms band around me, holding me close. "I love you."

I pull back and meet her eyes. "I had a really good proposal ready. Lots of fluffy and flowery words."

She nips at my bottom lip and then stares down at the four-carat diamond gleaming on her hand. "Yeah, but this is a really good story. One we'll tell our grandchildren all about."

"You mean how we turned a holiday fling into forever?"

"Does it get any better than that?"


THE END.


THANK you for reading my fun and dirty holiday romance! If you love fake relationship romances, check out my steamy, bestselling, billionaire, fake engagement romance, Doctor Scandalous. Turn the page to read an exclusive excerpt of Chapter one.

Want another of my Christmas books free? Click HERE.

## Doctor Scandalous

Oliver

I'M WALKING toward the gates of hell. And they charge for admission.

"Oh, Oliver..." Christa Foreman greets me with a slow once-over, her pastel-pink lips curling up into an impish grin. She's aptly named, because our senior class president was no joke when it came to strong-arming and manipulating her fellow classmates into getting what she wanted. "It's so good to see you. Wow. I mean, I see your pictures in magazines and on social media every now and then because I follow you, but you're way better looking in person than I remember from high school."

"Um. Thank you?" It comes out as a question, my head tilting in her direction.

"Sure. No problem." She licks her lips, her long, fake eyelashes batting faster than a butterfly's wings at me. "Are you here alone tonight?" She giggles as a flush creeps up her cheeks. She's married. Can we just say that? "I'm only asking because I need to know how much to charge you. I got stuck collecting money until the event coordinator can get her shit together." She huffs out a flustered breath, rolling her eyes derisively. "Anyway, it's a hundred per person. Should I put you down for one or two?"

And this is where I hesitate. Not over the money. The money is not an issue.

"Just give me a second."

Christa stares longingly at me, licking her lips. "Sure. I'll give you all night."

"Right." Because I have no idea what else to say to that. I don't remember Christa being so overtly interested in me when we were in high school. Then again, that was ten years ago, and I was most definitely taken. Which is both the main reason I don't want to be here and the main reason I came. But now I'm starting to reconsider everything.

I have nothing to prove by being here.

Not to *her*, her douchebag husband—my former friend— or anyone else.

I should just go. Maybe meet up with Carter, who I already know is going to our favorite bar, and get lost in a night of fun. Nothing about this hellhole will be fun. And in truth, I could really use a drink. A quiet one. It's been a shitful week. Too many patients. Not enough time. Oh, and finding out that your mom's cancer is back is always a winner.

I slip my phone from my pocket and shoot off a text to my best friend, Grace.

**Me: Sorry, babe. Not gonna be able to make it.**

The message bubble instantly dances along my screen. **Grace: It's not a choice, honey pie. Everyone is already asking when you're going to get here. Everyone.**

And instantly I'm tempted to ask if *she's* asking. In fact, my thumbs, who seem to have a mind of their own, start to type that very question until I tamp them down and rein them under control. Of course, she's asking. That's what she does.

She continues to hunt me down with terrorist-level determination, even all these years later.

She's likely giddy at the prospect of rubbing her picture-perfect life in my face without even caring that she's the last person on the planet I want to see tonight or any other night. Hence why now is the perfect time to leave.

**Me: Don't care.**

**Grace: Yes, you do. Come on. I know you're already dressed for tonight. Carter sent me a text.**

Carter. My traitorous brother.

**Grace: Just come inside the hotel. Come up to the reunion. Have a drink with me. See the people you haven't seen since high school who will fall at your feet the way they did back in the day. Oh wait, they still do.**

**Me: You're doing a shitty job of selling it there, sweetums.**

**Grace: Everyone will think you're a pussy if you don't come.**

**Me: Nice gauntlet drop.**

**Grace: I thought so. Now get your ass over here!**

I growl out a slew of curses under my breath, still seriously contemplating fleeing for the sake of my sanity, when I catch sight of a short, curvy redhead in a tight, backless black dress, higher than high heels, and fuck-me red lips that match her hair walking up to Christa. She's as late as I am, and before I know what I'm doing, a smile cracks clear across my face.

I know her instantly.

Even if it's been ten years since I've seen her. A guy never forgets the girl who gave him his first boner. A first-ever boner in class, I might add. We were twelve and she bent over to retrieve her fallen pencil when a flash of her training bra caught my eye. Instant erection.

I was pretty smitten after that moment, as you might imagine.

"Amelia," Christa greets her, her face now lacking any of the warmth it had when she was talking to me. "I had no idea you were coming."

What the fuck? You'd think in the ten years since we graduated from our annoyingly prestigious prep school that the rich girls would get over the self-created, mean-girl bullshit they had with the scholarship kids.

Amelia turns redder than her hair, and she takes a small step back before straightening her frame and squaring her shoulders. "Well, I'm here. Graduated same year as you. I even received the invitation in the mail. Must have been an error on your part," she finishes sarcastically.

"Uh-huh. It's a hundred-dollar entrance fee," Christa snaps, taking far too much pleasure in announcing that sum as she purses her lips off to the side, giving Amelia a nasty-girl slow once-over.

"A hundred dollars?" Amelia asks, though it comes out in a deflated, breathy whisper.

"Yup. Sorry," Christa sneers with a sorry-not-sorry saccharine sweet voice. "No exceptions. Not even for the kids who were on scholarship."

And that's it. Before Christa can say anything else that will make me want to throttle her, I walk over to Amelia, wrapping my hand around her waist. "Sweetheart," I exclaim. "You made it. I was starting to get worried."

Amelia jolts in my arms, her breath catching high in her throat as she twists to face me. Then she looks up and up a bit more because she's about a foot shorter than I am even in her heels. Suddenly, two sparkling gray eyes blink rapidly at me, and my heart starts to pound in time with the flutter of her lashes, my mouth dry like I've been eating sand all night.

"I'm sorry," she says, confused, her parted lips hanging just a bit too open for us to be selling this. "I think you must—"

I lean in, my nose brushing against her silky red hair that

smells like honeysuckle or something sweet and I breathe into her ear, "Just go with it."

She swallows audibly as I pull back, staring into her eyes and wondering how a color like that is even possible when she smiles and robs me of my breath. *Whoa*. That's unexpected.

"I didn't mean to worry you…" She trips up, biting into her lip like she's searching for a suitable term of endearment. Or maybe my name? I guess it is possible she has no idea who I am. We didn't exactly run in the same circles, and I just came up to her and wrapped my arm around her. "Oli," she finishes with, and I blow out the breath I didn't even realize I was holding.

"It's fine. I just didn't want to go in without the most beautiful woman in the world on my arm."

Amelia gives me that stunning smile again, this time with a blush staining her cheeks, and I marvel at how it makes her eyes glow to a smoky charcoal. Goddamn, she's fucking sexy.

"Wait," Christa interrupts. "You're with her?" She points at Amelia.

"I sure am," I declare without removing my eyes from Amelia's because those eyes, man. They're just too pretty not to stare at. "I'm a lucky bastard, right?"

"You're with him?" She turns that finger on me.

"So it seems," Amelia replies, her tone a bit bewildered, though there is a hint of amusement in there, too.

"But. You're. You. No. You're Oliver Fritz," Christa sputters incredulously. "And she's Amelia——" Her words cut off when I throw her my most menacing glare, already knowing the exact nasty nickname she's about to throw out. Why certain women feel the need to degrade and belittle other women, I'll never understand.

I slip two one-hundred-dollar bills from my wallet and toss them at Christa. "Have a good night," I say instead of what I'm really thinking. My fingers intertwine with Amelia's, and then I'm dragging her past Christa, down the long corridor with the paisley rug and gold walls, toward the ballroom.

I guess I'm going to my high school reunion after all.

The second we're out of sight of Christa, Amelia yanks her hand from mine, stopping in the middle of the hall and turning to stare up at me. "You remember me?" she asks and then shakes her head like that's not what she meant to say.

"Amelia Atkins. You were in most of my classes from the time we were in sixth grade or so, on."

"Right. What I meant to say is, thank you for stepping in back there, but it really wasn't necessary."

"Maybe not. I'm sure you can handle yourself with women like Christa. But it felt wrong to stand there and watch that go down, doing nothing. I can't stand women who feel the need to hurt others just to make themselves look and feel better."

She folds her arms over her chest, giving me a raised eyebrow. "And yet you dated a woman who did exactly that all through high school."

Touché. A bark of a laugh slips out my lungs. "Can't argue with that. Hell, I dated that same vicious woman through college too. Adolescent mistake. What can I say?"

Still, at the mention of that particular woman, an old flair hits me straight in the chest. My fingers find my pocket, toying with the large diamond solitaire set in a diamond and platinum band I stuck in there tonight. It's *the* ring. The one I nearly gave to said woman who was screwing around on me with my friend, Rob. A lesson in betrayal I've never forgotten. It's why on certain occasions, I carry it with me.

A reminder to never get too close again.

"Sorry," Amelia says, withering before my eyes. "That was insanely rude of me. I don't even know why I said that. Christa got my hackles all fired up, and I just took them out on you instead of her, like I should have. Damn, some women seriously suck, right?" I can't stop my chuckle, though I think she was being serious. She stares down at the rug, shifting her stance until she's leaning back against the wall opposite the closed doors where the reunion is taking place. "Look, I wish you hadn't paid for me. Money and I aren't exactly on speaking terms at the moment. It's going to take me a while to pay you back. But I *will* pay you back. I just don't have that kind of—"

My fingers latch on to her chin, tilting her head back up until our eyes meet. "I don't care about the money. And I don't want you to pay me back." She opens her mouth as if to argue with me, and I shake my head, cutting her off again. "I mean it."

She huffs out a breath. "Well, thank you. That's very generous. But if this is how this night is already starting off, I'm thinking maybe I should just go. Hell, I shouldn't even have come here in the first place. I don't know what I was thinking. My sister talked me into it, and I thought…" She shakes her head. "Never mind. It's stupid."

I prop my shoulder against the wall so I'm facing her, folding my arms while I stare at her because I can't seem to help myself. "Why is it stupid?"

"You really want to know?"

"I really want to know."

Those big eyes slay through me, slightly glassy with emotion. "Because no one in there wants me there. You heard Christa. I was fooling myself into thinking that I could waltz in here ten years later and everyone who treated me like garbage growing up would finally see me for me. That they'd finally realize we're all on an even playing field now that high school is over. It was going to be like putting all my old bully nightmares to rest once and for all. Only, nothing has changed. I'm still the girl wearing thrift store digs who couldn't even afford to pay the entrance fee."

Wow. That's…

"Can I tell you something?" I ask.

Her hands meet her hips. "You mean something to rival the way too personal verbal diarrhea I just spouted at a man I haven't seen in a decade?"

She's trying for brave and strong, and even sarcastic. But she's sad. I can see it in her eyes that bounce around my face, almost as if she's not sure she wants to know what I'm about to say. No one wants to be slammed back into their high school nightmare. She wanted to walk in there and make all those assholes eat their words.

I want that for her too.

I like Amelia. I always have. There was something about her that just got to me on a weird level I never quite understood. She was sweet and nerdy and quiet and reserved. So understatedly beautiful. Her hair was all wild with red curls. Her glasses a touch too big for her face. Her body small with her ample curves hidden beneath her ill-fitting prep school uniform.

And looking at her now, after hearing what Christa was saying to her…

In truth, I do remember people being that nasty. Though now I'm positive it was a lot worse than I knew about if Christa's reaction to her tonight is anything to go by. I only heard comments here and there that I didn't pay much attention to, nor did anything to stop. Even if I never directly contributed to it, by not stopping it, I was part of the problem.

That's on me. And it's not okay. I should have done more to protect her. I should have said something.

"Something like that. You told me yours. Now I'll tell you mine."

"Alright."

I step into her, bending down like I'm about to tell her a secret when really, I just want to be closer to her. Smell her shampoo that makes my cock jump in my slacks. Feel the heat of her body as she starts to blush from my proximity.

"I don't want to be here either. I got talked into it by my friend, Grace, and now here I am."

Her eyebrows knit together. "Why wouldn't you want to be here? You're a doctor. You were the most popular guy in our class. Captain of the football team. Everyone loved you. Still do, if the tabloids are anything to go by."

I suck in a deep breath, ready to tell her something only my family and Grace know. "My ex is not only in there with her husband, my former friend, but she's pregnant. Likely going to be delivered by either my brother or my best friend since she sought them out to be her OB. How's that for irony?" I roll my eyes. "The only saving grace I have when it comes to Nora is that she never knew I was about to propose. I had the ring in my pocket, ready to drop down onto one knee, but before I could do anything, she told me she was in love with Rob and that we were over."

Amelia sucks in a rush of air, her eyes flashing. Her hand shoots up, covering her parted lips as she stares at me with a combination of shock and sympathy. "God. That's awful."

"The real kicker of all that is I had made a lot of sacrifices for her. A lot. Nearly everything I wanted I had given up for her with the exception of medicine. But I chose NYU to be with her instead of playing ball at Michigan. I finished college in three years instead of four because she said the sooner I can complete med school and residency, the better. Then, on the fucking day I got into Columbia for med school and was set to propose, she informed me she had been cheating on me for the better half of six months."

Six. Fucking. Months!

"Jesus, Oliver. I'm so sorry. I never heard anything about that."

"That's because no one knows, so if you wouldn't mind keeping that to yourself, I'd appreciate it. The last thing I want is for that to hit the press next."

She reaches out her hand, touching my arm and giving

me a squeeze. "Of course. I'll never tell anyone. I don't blame you for not wanting to go in there. It seems we both felt like we had something to prove by showing up tonight."

That's not the reason I came tonight. But Nora is the main reason I didn't want to go in. I've successfully avoided seeing her for years. In truth, I've been over her for a long time, just not over what she did to me. Most of my bitterness and resentment is on me. I should never have made those sacrifices for her.

I gave up pieces of myself I can never get back.

But Amelia deserves more. She always has, and she never got it. She deserves to have people look at her and treat her with the respect they never did. They owe it to her. Hell, I owe it to her. I don't want her to leave tonight the way she is now.

"I only wish it had turned out better for us," she continues. "But I think my carriage has officially turned back into a pumpkin and I should just cut my losses and head home. Tonight can't possibly end the way I had envisioned it."

Like a bolt of electricity flowing through me, suddenly I'm giddy with an idea that is quite possibly the most ridiculous idea in the history of ideas. Christa nearly swallowed her tongue when she thought Amelia was my date. So maybe everyone else will react the same way if that's what they see. Bonus for me—I'll have a hot as hell woman on my arm and maybe Nora will leave me alone.

More than that, I *want* to go in there with Amelia. I want to spend more time with her tonight. And if they don't like it or think less of me for it, well, I don't give a shit.

But Amelia being my date isn't enough. Not with my reputation. They'll just assume I'm using her, because ever since Nora and I split up... I've been somewhat of a player. A fact the media loves to report on. Hell, my face is splashed across the internet every other week, showing me with a different woman each time. Not in the last few months or so, but it's been the standard of my life since Nora. It's the way I keep from getting hurt again.

And the media reporting on it all? Well, that's the standard of all my brothers' lives. It comes with being a Fritz and living in Boston. We own this city. We're royalty. For better or worse, that's how it is.

But if Amelia and I really want to make an impact tonight… if I really want to make all those assholes who hurt Amelia choke, and Nora—who still calls me to tell me *all* her 'happy' news—realize that I've finally and officially moved on from her… it needs to be more than just people thinking I'm dating Amelia.

They need to know she's something special. Believe she's something special *to me*.

My fingers dig back into my pocket, locating that ring. Looking at her… plotting this insane idea… I'm hit with the fact that I know it will change everything. Both for her and for me.

A deviously crooked smile curls up at the corner of my lips.

Yeah. I have an idea, alright. And I think I can get Amelia to go for it. It's only for a few hours anyway. What could go wrong?

WANT to find out what happens next with Oliver and Amelia in this fake engagement, single parent, billionaire romance? Get your copy of Doctor Scandalous today.

Made in United States
Troutdale, OR
10/06/2024

23462551R00105